PRAISE FOR
THE PAIN OF OTHERS

"An absorbing book of unwavering honesty. A magnificent novel without fiction."
—Javier Cercas, author of *Soldiers of Salamis*

"The author as host and guest in his own story. A meditation on writing, a friend who murders his sister then takes his own life, who appears out of the blue in a photograph, an investigation, a portrait of Spain in the nineties and, in short, an outstanding novel by Miguel Ángel Hernández."
—Fernando Aramburu, author of *Homeland*

"A unique, powerful, and brutal novel."
—*Qué Leer*

"A work as harrowing as it is empathetic—raw and beautiful."
—*Rockdelux*

"A magnificent autobiographical text, full of pain and unanswered questions."
—*Les Inrockuptibles*

"A moving book, written with exquisite intelligence and sensitivity. A treatise on inappropriate affections and the failure to understand evil when it appears in our communities and takes root in those we love—on empathy, the power of language, and its limits."

—*El País*

PRAISE FOR
ANOXIA

"The macabre and stimulating story of a woman drawn into the world of mortuary photography... Dolores's uncanny feelings build as her town is plagued by floods, giving this exploration of grief a gravitas that edges on the gothic, even as Hernández's style remains sober and satisfyingly understated. This will linger in readers' minds."

—*Publishers Weekly*

"Moody and multilayered, this novel, like its photography subjects, has earned a long and eerie afterlife."

—*CrimeReads*, Best International Fiction of the Month

"*Anoxia* is a lovely, dark, delicately written meditation on grief."

—Erika T. Wurth, author of *White Horse*

"It was with great anticipation that I picked up *Anoxia*. Hernández has style, depth, humor, penetrating intelligence, and a profound insight of pathos and the modern fable. *Anoxia* is all at once the endless fall and the endless flight, a shared memory and an entirely new experience."

—John Reed, author of *Snowball's Chance*

"Today, the old art of portraying the dead is disappearing. This novel is a powerful creation that draws on both the materiality of photography and the enigmas of death. Photography is different from the images of our digital age, and its outcome—memory—deals as much with the past as with the present. Death, the source of our work of mourning, does not simply mean loss, since it engenders a new relationship with the dead, who continue haunting our lives. With *Anoxia*, Walter Benjamin, Roland Barthes, and Susan Sontag have found a literary companion capable of dialoguing with them. An amazing accomplishment."

—Enzo Traverso, author of *Gaza Faces History*

"Set on the storm-lashed Mediterranean coast, *Anoxia* is a powerful, atmospheric novel that explores grief, art, and the transformative power of creation. As floodwaters reshape the land, Dolores—paralyzed by the loss of her husband—seeks solace in the lost art of daguerreotype photography, which captures not just a tangible image, but the shimmering essence of a moment in time. Dolores begins working with a mysterious older man who collects postmortem images, and learns that by capturing death, she is, paradoxically, reclaiming her own life. In this luminous novel, we follow the story of her awakening. A daringly original novel by one of the most gifted writers of the vibrant contemporary Spanish scene, *Anoxia* is a gorgeous meditation on the human experience, where art becomes both a vessel for grief and a source of profound, transformational beauty."

—Valerie Miles, author of
A Thousand Forests in One Acorn

"Miguel Ángel Hernández writes novels that integrate a gripping fabula with one or more important theoretical issues. While reading the engaging story, the reader cannot help but absorb relevant ideas about social-political reality as well as aesthetic questions. The literary quality matches the level of thinking. In *Anoxia* this concerns the combination of the art of photography with the personal effort of memory. Once you read all his novels you will have acquired unique insights that are indispensable but difficult to learn through teaching and studying."

—Mieke Bal, author of *Narratology* and *Quoting Caravaggio*

"An enthralling story about photography, and the limits between life and death."

—*ABC Cultural*

"In *Anoxia* . . . [Hernández] has achieved the perfect equilibrium . . . The tradition of mortuary photography drives a mysterious plot that flirts with the thriller, though the greatest value lies in the subtlety with which Hernández tackles the emotional consequences of grief."

—*El Cultural*

THE PAIN OF OTHERS

ALSO BY MIGUEL ÁNGEL HERNÁNDEZ

Anoxia

THE PAIN OF OTHERS

MIGUEL ÁNGEL HERNÁNDEZ

Translated from the Spanish by Adrian Nathan West

OTHER PRESS | NEW YORK

Originally published in Spanish as *El dolor de los demás* in 2018 by
Editorial Anagrama, Barcelona

Published in agreement with Casanovas & Lynch Literary Agency

Production editor: Yvonne E. Cárdenas
Text designer: Patrice Sheridan
This book was set in Galliard and Futura by
Alpha Design & Composition of Pittsfield, NH

1 3 5 7 9 10 8 6 4 2

 Printed in the United States of America on acid-free paper. For information write to Other Press LLC, 267 Fifth Avenue, 6th Floor, New York, NY 10016.
Or visit our Web site: www.otherpress.com

Library Of Congress Cataloging-in-Publication Data
Names: Hernández, Miguel Ángel, 1977- author |
West, Adrian Nathan translator
Title: The pain of others : a novel / Miguel Ángel Hernández ;
translated from the Spanish by Adrian Nathan West.
Other titles: Dolor de los demás. English
Description: New York : Other Press, 2026.
Identifiers: LCCN 2025042675 (print) | LCCN 2025042676 (ebook) |
ISBN 9781635424607 paperback | ISBN 9781635424614 ebook
Subjects: LCGFT: Fiction | Novels
Classification: LCC PQ6708.E765 D6513 2026 (print) |
LCC PQ6708.E765 (ebook)
LC record available at https://lccn.loc.gov/2025042675
LC ebook record available at https://lccn.loc.gov/2025042676

Publisher's Note

This is a work of fiction. Names, characters, places, and incidents either are the product of the author's imagination or are used fictitiously.

To Julia—the *Julia*—

for love, for life, for all of it

Memory is, achingly,
the only relation
we can have
with the dead.

—SUSAN SONTAG

I

TWENTY YEARS

SOMEONE BROKE INTO Rosario's house, killed Rosi, and kidnapped Nicolás, you hear your father say in the other room.

It's the first thing you hear. A voice that awakens you. A phrase you'll never forget.

For a moment, you try to tell yourself it's a dream. You remain there, paralyzed, in the sheets. It's five in the morning, and you've barely slept a wink. Your Christmas Eve dinner didn't go down well, and for hours, you've been tossing and turning in bed.

They killed Rosi and they took Nicolás, you hear your father say clearly now.

That's when you open your eyes, still baffled, jump out of bed, throw on the clothing that lies nearest to hand and run off to the living room.

Your mother's in her nightgown next to the Christmas tree. She looks at you and starts to cry.

Rosario's children . . . , she manages to say.

What happened? you ask.

Something bad, she responds, something bad, son. And she brings her hands to her face to hide her tears.

Your father's in the bathroom getting dressed. Your brother, the first to hear the news, is standing in the doorway trying to hurry him along.

He walks out and tells you, Come along if you feel like it.

Your mother stays home. You go with them.

Be careful, she warns. And lock the door behind you.

The cold sinks into your bones and the damp into your brain. It's December in the lowlands of Murcia.

The three of you walk down the dark road in silence. A soft roar absorbs every sound, and it grows as you approach the road, walking in the direction of the driveway, which is dense with silhouettes that then dissolve in the morning shadows.

Soft light from a cracked fixture lights up the bystanders' faces. No one looks at each other, and everyone speaks softly.

Three patrol cars are blocking the entrance to the house. Beside them, alone, pacing in small circles with his hands behind his back, is your friend's father.

What happened, Antón? your brother asks as you approach him.

Nothing . . . , he murmurs, eyes trained on the ground, just that they've killed my Rosi and taken Nicolás with them.

This is all he says, and he repeats it over and over: to the neighbor from across the street, to your neighbor Julia, to your cousin Maruja, to anyone who stops their car and comes over and asks. He says it with that same lost look in his eyes, expression unhinged, incredulous, as if he didn't really know what happened, as if nothing had happened at all.

Nothing.

That's the word he begins with every time someone asks.

And that is what no one understands. This nothing that can't be said. This nothing that creeps into every crook and corner. This nothing that immobilizes you and clouds your mind. This nothing, and two questions:

Who killed Rosi?

Who took Nicolás away?

1

"**TWENTY YEARS AGO,** on Christmas Eve, my best friend killed his sister and threw himself off a cliff."

"Don't overthink it, man. You've got the story you were looking for right there."

The author Sergio del Molino had come to Murcia to present his book *What No One Cares About*, and I had just told him that the story he recounts in that novel, the reconstruction of his maternal grandfather's life, had left me without ideas for my own upcoming project. I was busy writing my second novel, and over the past few months, I had sketched out a few pages about my father's father. At the beginning of summer, one of my uncles had come back to Spain from Argentina after several decades away. My brothers had organized a family lunch, and he had hypnotized us with the story of my grandfather Cristóbal. According to my uncle, his father was one of Franco's spies in Africa, feared in Guadix for his savagery after the war. He kidnapped my grandmother soon after she'd turned twelve and took most of his family to Argentina to seek his fortune. No sooner than they'd arrived, he abandoned them all, and they knew nothing of what had happened to him until the mid-seventies, when they found his body in a ditch on the side of a country road.

Once or twice, I'd heard my father talk about my grandfather's character, his sternness, the way, in the postwar years, the Civil Guards stood at attention in his presence, and even how he'd jumped over the wall around my grandmother's backyard to spirit her away by force. He probably told that story about Argentina that I heard from his brother years later, but I don't remember, and maybe I wasn't paying attention. Children just don't pay attention to their parents. And they don't realize it until it's too late. Maybe for that reason—and maybe too because, despite my uncle's strong Argentine accent, his voice reminded me of my father—I followed his story that afternoon as if it were *The Thousand and One Nights.* And when he finished and paused and exclaimed, "That son of a bitch, Grandpa Cristóbal," I felt the urge to delve into the life of that stranger I'd never even seen a photo of.

For months, the idea grew in my head. I opened a notebook and started filling it with notes, drafts, ideas. I even considered abandoning the novel I was writing at the time. But at the end of the summer of 2014, just when I had well and truly decided that my next book would try to trace out the exploits of this cruel, infamous ancestor, Sergio del Molino's book arrived at my home and spoiled all my plans. He had written the book I wanted to write. The lives in question were different—his grandfather wasn't a miserable bastard the way mine seems to have been—but what I wanted to tell—the story of a country and a generation seen through the life of a single person—was the very heart of Sergio's book. And so writing this after him didn't make much sense. Not then, anyway. And so when I saw him in Murcia a few months later, I couldn't help but say, "You fucker, you stole my next novel from me."

And it was then, after a conversation about autofiction, nonfiction, novels based on true events, and autobiographies, that I mentioned a story, not the one about my grandfather, but another one that I'd been holding on to for a long time. A bitter story, one I wasn't sure I'd ever have the courage to face, but which I summarized in one raw, dry phrase: "Twenty years ago, on Christmas Eve, my best friend killed his sister and threw himself off a cliff."

Those words contained a story. The past I've sought to escape from my entire life.

Twenty years ago . . .

I had just turned eighteen, I was living with my parents in a small village in the Murcian lowlands, and I had begun studying art history at the university. My father packaged windows in an aluminum workshop, and my mother was taking care of Nena, her aunt, who was past ninety and spent her days sitting there and looking out the window. My three brothers, who all married when I was still a kid, had left home some time ago. I would stay there, though, in the middle of nowhere, for some time, with Nena and my parents, who were so much older than I, they could easily have been my grandparents.

I was coddled, spoiled, the baby. I had everything my parents and brothers never could. And that meant I had no right to complain, because I didn't know what it meant to work like a dog or scrounge money just to eat. And so I had to study, try my best, take advantage of that opportunity everyone else had been forced to pass up. Study so you don't end up working in the fields. Get a certificate in whatever, accounting, automotive engineering, electronics. Or better, take the college track, pass your exams, and if you're lucky, you get into university. You can study whatever. Ideally law, or education, or psychology. Even art history. That was still a degree. And a degree was a future. I was the first person in my family to go to college. What a source of pride. All their efforts, all that overtime, all those sleepless nights, they were finally worth it. *My son, the college graduate*, was what my mother yearned to say, *he shuts himself in his room to study and hardly ever sees the light of day, but someday, he's going to be somebody.*

Her son—me—was for the moment just a fat kid. A fat kid and not much else. A fat kid with hang-ups who bought black T-shirts two sizes too big so no one would notice his love handles. A studious fat kid, but invisible, who passed unnoticed through elementary school and high school and still had no idea that he'd one day show a knack for memorizing slides of Greek temples and Baroque paintings. A fat kid who hadn't written a single line, who hadn't even hit on the notion of becoming a writer. A fat kid who read till his eyes ached and compulsively devoured whatever book fell into his hands.

That was me. The fat kid who read in a world where no one else did. In my house, there were no books until I started showing up with them. First they were loaners, from the library at school; then from the libraries in the surrounding towns; finally, I started buying books of my own. At the bookstore in the village and the kiosk in the square. New books and secondhand ones. Classic and contemporary. Dostoevsky and Stephen King. Hermann Hesse and Dean R. Koontz. I didn't have standards. Or my standard was simply: Books are good, all of them, and they all need to be read. And that's what I did. I read till my eyes burned and my vision was blurry. Until reality vanished and a different world opened before me. Like those nights I spent in a kitchen chair with *The Little Vampire* when I was eight years old and still didn't have my own room. Or the week I bundled up in the quilt on the sofa to read *The Neverending Story* two times through, like Bastian Balthazar Bux, illuminating the pages with the same square flashlight my father took out at night when the men went to water their lemon trees.

I think about it now, and that image seems like a condensation of my two worlds. The world under the quilt on the sofa and the world outside. The universe of books and life in the lowlands. The place I wanted to flee to and the place where I was forced to live, a small old world, closed, claustrophobic, where the very air was heavy.

In 1995—the *twenty years ago* of the phrase printed above—I set out on my own private attempt to escape, though I didn't yet know it. College, the city, the world beyond the lowlands—that would be my salvation. There, I would find a place I belonged. The place I should have been born. But there were burdens still that wouldn't let me leave and that kept me bound to that territory I returned to every afternoon. One of these had been my shadow, my source of oxygen in the past, the boy I grew up next to: Nicolás, Rosario's kid, my neighbor on the farm. I'd put some distance between us, but I still considered him...

...my best friend.

We lived no more than six hundred feet from each other. His house was on a slight elevation and bordered the road that cut through the lowlands. My home was at the end of a gravel road. Both were surrounded by lemon groves. The same pattern hemmed us both in. Nicolás was a few weeks younger than I, the son of older parents, like me, the youngest of four siblings. He had one sister. In my family, we were all boys. And he and I were two peas in a pod. Thick as thieves. Inseparable. I was squat and tubby, he was tall and thin. I had fat cheeks and pink skin; he was coppery, sloe-eyed, with hard features and glimmers in his black hair.

When I think about him, I don't know why, I always imagine him in a purplish nylon tracksuit. I remember him being sort of lost, quiet, self-absorbed, taciturn. Indeed, that was what defined Nicolás. If I was a fat toiler, he was sickly and timid. Today, I imagine they'd have diagnosed him with something on the autism spectrum. Back then he was a *quiet kid*, withdrawn and prone to embarrassment. A weird kid who kept his head down and spoke in little more than a whisper. He was that way when he was four, and he was that way when he was seventeen.

He didn't act like the rest of the kids. He was special. When people made fun of him, he could take it, better than anyone else could, but there was a limit. Once you passed it, he exploded. The rage he'd been holding back burst out. And that strength of his—no one knew where it came from. Those fleeting instants of rage surprised even me. I had been his voice, his shield. I spoke for him and protected him. Next to him, I felt powerful. I ruled and he obeyed. He was my double, and probably my lackey.

He was always there in my life, from the first day of kindergarten to the night when everything happened. It's true that our paths forked after elementary school: He went vocational, I prepared for college. We no longer saw each other in class anymore, but we'd meet in the afternoons on the fields to play soccer, basketball, pachisi, cards, or video games. Then there were Sundays at the chapel. Preparing for the readings, helping with Mass. And catechism and confirmation classes in the next village over on Friday afternoons and Saturday mornings.

Until the last time I saw him, on December 24, 1995, sitting at the gate, playing chess with his cousin Pedro Luis a few hours before the night when...

...he killed his sister and threw himself off a cliff.

That night, after Christmas Eve dinner, around two in the morning, when his parents were in bed and the rest of the family was gone, Nicolás went into Rosi's room and beat her until her life was over. He bludgeoned her with a tape player—or, some say, with a metal scale—or with any and everything he could grab. Their parents didn't hear the blows or the screams. It was the sound of the car starting that woke them. When they went to their daughter's bedroom, they found her body laid out in a puddle of blood.

They looked for Nicolás, but he was gone. His car, a blue Seat 127, had vanished too. They called the Civil Guard, and soon, the search was underway. No one knew where he might have gone. A few hours later, as day broke, they found his body in El Cabezo de la Plata, the rocky hill country around seven miles from his home. His cousin Juan Alberto, another of my best friends, spotted it at the bottom of a gulley. Nicolás had a belt around his neck. He'd tried to strangle himself before jumping.

Those were the facts. Everything I knew, everything I'd managed to find out in the aftermath. If I ever dared to write that story, it would have to begin with that.

Making everything plain from the beginning. He killed her, and that same night, he killed himself. There is no more intrigue, no more mystery. Or rather, that was the mystery: Why did he kill her? What was going through his mind? How did the fight start? Was there a fight? Had they fought before? What could have turned a holiday evening into a dreadful nightmare?

There was no explanation. Everyone said they were a normal family, with good kids, I said this too, to the media and to the Civil Guards. No one knew anything. And no one has learned anything since. The case was closed, and the questions remained unanswered. The secret became an enigma, and the solution was buried forever with those two young people's bodies. The facts, those were the only clear things: There was one victim and one killer. And the killer too was dead. Everything else was pure speculation.

Strange as it may seem, I hardly looked back on that bitter night. I preferred to clear it from my mind and flee, moving on as if nothing had ever happened. I was eighteen, an adolescent, and it should have torn me up inside. But instead, I turned the page in a way that, when I think about it, surprises me and that I struggle to understand.

Over time, that long night turned into just another story from my past. An episode I never delved into beyond that phrase I repeated like a mantra: *My best friend killed his sister and threw himself off a cliff.* A formula that was perhaps like armor, protection against that darkness I'd never known how to penetrate.

And yet, in that phrase, that formula, that armor I had built to isolate myself from my past and my past from my present, there was a story to be told. That was what Sergio had suggested. Others before him had done the same. You need to write this down someday, my friend Leo said every time the subject came up. Yeah, someday, I'd say, thinking how that day would recede into the distance forever while I remained absorbed in artists, intellectuals, and theories.

Someday, I'd think. Someday I'll go back to that night and everything will come back with it: Nicolás, life in the lowlands, my origins, my home, my parents, the neighbors, the absence of understanding, that universe I had emerged from and that I'd never wanted to return to. Someday, I told myself. Someday I'll write about all my fears and frustrations and all the grief of my past.

Someday, I thought. Someday, I said. And in my heart, I was terrified that the someday always displaced into the future might break into the present and shatter it.

YOU HEAR THEM say: They took him away in the car. The kid. In his own car, they say.

The 127 isn't in the driveway. And when you arrived, the first thing you thought was: Did the killers force him to drive them?

You hardly have time to answer before someone grabs you by the shoulder.

Get him out of here, Julia, your father tells the neighbor.

Come on, son.

Take him away, your father repeats.

He and your brother Juan go into Rosario's house. They walk down the hall toward the place where it all happened. You depart from the scene.

Come on, son, Julia says again. I made you a lemon blossom tea. You could use it.

She takes you to the house next door, which shares a wall with your friend's place.

Lock the door, she says when you enter. They still haven't found them. Shut the door and lock it, please.

You realize then that the lemon blossom tea isn't for you. She's the one who's scared. Julia. Your neighbor. Your second mother.

You accept the cup of tea and look out the window.

The men are busy in the driveway. The women are asleep at home. The men are where everything's happening. And you want to be with them. With the men, not with the women. You wish you could go outside and leave Julia there.

You're not a child anymore. You're eighteen. But in the lowlands, that means nothing.

2

THERE WAS A story there. A novel maybe. The night I got home after Sergio del Molino's book presentation, I saw that possibility clearly. The euphoria of the gin-and-tonics we'd swilled down to celebrate our friendship had helped. The next morning, though, my hangover and the intrusion of reality slowly convinced me that I'd gotten ahead of myself. Where was I planning on going with this book? Was it supposed to be a true crime novel? A family story set in the lowlands of Murcia? That was unlike anything I'd done before. I had published a novel about the contemporary art world, and I was trying to finish another that dealt with the same subject: Artists, intellectuals, international exhibitions, recondite theories about the limits of representation and images and memory . . . that was what I knew how to write about. Delude myself as I might with this notion that I was a novelist, I remained a mere college professor who had drawn on his insights into his field to write in novel form what would otherwise have been the subject of an essay. And that was what I should keep doing. Sticking to what I knew and leaving everything else alone. Trying to put to paper the story

I'd told Sergio meant distancing myself from a relatively comfortable terrain and traveling toward the unknown, plunging into places I'd never gone before. Or that's what I thought at the time, at least. Now I know that everything's part of the same impulse and that in reality I wasn't veering away too far. But at that moment, I was convinced that it was a new path, and I wasn't sure I wanted to travel down it.

I spent most of the day tossing over these ideas. And I was still doing so when, in the afternoon, as I was waiting for the light to change before crossing the street after an uncomfortable department meeting, I noticed a car flashing its lights at me as someone waved from inside. I recognized the driver's face immediately: Juan Alberto. I hadn't seen him in nearly ten years. Someone had texted me that he was working in the police station nearby in Barrio del Carmen, but since my wedding, I'd hardly heard from him.

I walked over and waved back at him through the passenger window.

"We should catch up one of these days," he said, grabbing my forearm and looking into the rearview mirror.

"Definitely. Call me anytime."

"You should see my daughter. She's all grown up now. We've got shared custody."

I nodded.

"Good to see you, Miguel."

That's all we had time for. The light turned green and his car headed off into the city.

I was happy to see him too. But running into him just as I was starting to think about writing about what had happened twenty years before was a strange twist of fate. Not just because Juan Alberto had been one of my closest friends when I was a teenager and had sent me straight back into my past, but because he had played a fundamental role in the story I was considering. Juan Alberto was Nicolás's first cousin. He had known him well. And there was another thing: The night everything happened, after hours of searching, he was the one who had found the body in the gulley.

Funny enough, we'd never talked about that. Since that sad night, we'd never spent much time together at all. And even if there were other motives for the distance, what happened on that Christmas Eve in 1995 had also raised a wall of darkness between us, a zone not to be crossed, where everything had remained unsaid.

And now, when, for the first time in ages, I had admitted the possibility of looking back, Juan Alberto showed up again. What was the likelihood of that happening on that very afternoon? I've never really believed in destiny, but as I watched his car vanish into the distance, the naive idea passed through my head that someone or something had placed him in my path that day.

I think it was then that I convinced myself that I had to write this book. And it was then, too, that I became aware of what it would mean to do it, the wounds I'd reopen, the damage I could do.

Today, much later, with this book underway, in the knowledge that there is no turning back, it strikes me that Juan Alberto appeared that day not to convince me that this was the story I needed to tell, but on the contrary, to dissuade me, to warn me that there were waters it was best not to stir, places it was best not to enter; that not all stories need to be told, that writing isn't always a triumph, that sometimes, we too may founder upon the pain of others.

A KNOCK COMES at the door. Your father's face is yellow and his eyes are red. He needs into the bathroom. Coming out, Julia asks:

Do they know anything, Juan Antonio?

They killed the girl and Nicolás is gone.

They look at each other. She offers him a glass of lemon blossom tea. Lemon blossom tea, that cures everything. It's the antidote to fear.

No one knows anything, he says with his glass in his hand. The killers got away, and Nicolás is gone. He's disappeared, but they don't think he was kidnapped.

There's no justice in this world, your father says.

And he takes a drink of his tea.

Stay here. Don't go out. He adds this before leaving.

Ay, Nicolás, Julia sighs.

He's the only thing you can think of. Nicolás. Where is he? Did he manage to get away?

You don't ask about his sister. How Rosi was killed. Who killed her. Why. All you want to know is what happened to Nicolás. Is he hiding, is he on the run?

Ay, Nicolás, Julia says again.

And you notice something strange in her words, a timbre that is not just grief. And for a moment, you have the sensation that everything is condensed in this lament.

3

IN MID-NOVEMBER 2014, a month after my conversation with Sergio del Molino, my oldest brother's father-in-law died. He had been in the hospital a few days, then he stopped breathing. He was almost eighty, but we thought of him as the strongest person in the family. He had even taken care of his wife when she was bed-bound after a hip operation. This same wife would die a few months later, from grief or from the inability to understand how life can take a turn from one moment to the next and everything can change irrevocably. My sister-in-law, an only child, became an orphan in a matter of five months.

Her father's death was like a hammer blow. I was in class when I learned of it, and I took off for the funeral home, trying to get there as quickly as possible. I felt guilty. He'd had a brain hemorrhage, and I had only gone to the hospital to visit him once, and it had reminded me so much of my father's last days in the ICU, intubated and with no possibility of recovery, that I'd left the room for a breath of fresh air and burst into tears. I'd been overwhelmed with work and other commitments after that, and I hadn't called my sister-in-law to see how her father was. And so, the day he died, I wanted to be one of the first to show up.

The funeral home in Alquerías was built on the outside of town, surrounded by lemon trees, maybe two miles from where my brothers live to this day. When my father died, it was still in the planning phase, and we'd had to hold his viewing in the city. With my mother, it was quicker: Just a few minutes lay between the house where she collapsed and the refrigerated chamber with the window in it where we observed her for one day and one night. I wrote a book to keep myself from forgetting those bitter moments. My notebook about death and mourning. Writing threw up a barrier. Words stanched my emotions. And now, as I write this paragraph, it strikes me that this book, too, is full of dead people. Dead people and places of mourning. It is, once again, a tragic text. Death reclaims its place in everything I write.

At the door to the funeral home, I found my brother Emilio and his wife. They, too, had arrived early.

"Are you writing?" my sister-in-law Mari Carmen asked. She's the only one in the family who was interested in my books, and she asked about them every time she saw me. She'd never published anything, and all she read was romance novels, but she'd tried her hand at a story or two and had aspirations of one day writing a novel of her own.

"I'm working on something, yeah," I answered. But instead of talking to her about the novel I was pecking at, I confessed, "I actually started writing something about Rosi and Nicolás."

Her expression changed drastically. She had known Rosi well, they had gone out partying together a few times.

"You can't do that," she replied hesitantly. "He was a murderer. And you never managed to see that."

"I'm going to tell what happened."

"What—that he was a son of a bitch?" she asked. "Because that's what happened. That's what you have to write."

"Hush," my brother interrupted her. "He knows what he needs to write. He's the one who went to college, remember?"

As we spoke, other neighbors began arriving. One of them walked over and my brother greeted him effusively.

"Hey... Garre."

Garre owned a lemon warehouse where my brothers worked a few summers when they were young. My mother used to talk sometimes about how he won them over with his jokes and his sense of humor, even if he only paid them a pittance.

"So you're the little brother?" Garre said, turning to me. "Look at that lily-white skin of his. I'm guessing you don't put in too many hours out in the fields?"

I tried to smile. I was used to these remarks. For a few seconds, the sight of his floral-patterned shirt absorbed me, with the open collar and the huge gold chain that seemed to float over his curly white chest hairs.

"He's a writer," my brother responded, sarcastic but also proud. "He's starting a book about what happened in the lowlands, the murder, Rosario's kids, you know."

"Shit," the man exclaimed. "There's a lot to chew on there. Those two apparently had something going on."

"What are you talking about?" my sister-in-law butted in.

"That's what people say. Seems she was also pregnant by him."

"That's ridiculous, and you're taking it too far," she responded.

Garre objected, "Everyone knows it..."

"That's a lie," Mari Carmen told him, then looked at me directly. "Your brother Juan saw her maxi pad, it had blood on it, she was on her period. He told me so."

Her eyes were damp, and she took out a Kleenex to wipe away the tears.

"Don't get like that," Garre said, trying and failing to console her. "It's just weird to me that y'all live so close and don't know what all people say about it."

"What do they say?" I asked.

"Lots of stuff. I don't know. Like that his brothers are the ones who chased him to El Cabezo and pushed him off the cliff."

"I never heard that," I said.

"How the hell would you hear it, you don't live here," Garre responded. Then he remarked to my brother, "This intellectual here... he sure doesn't seem like your brother." He turned back to me. "Kid, you don't know nothing. There's more to all this than people said at the time. Lots more."

I didn't even have time to get indignant at his tone as he called me *intellectual* before the hearse arrived, and behind it, my brother José Antonio with his wife and two kids. I approached to give my condolences as they got out of the car. Once back in the funeral home, I sat in one of the chairs set out to keep vigil for the deceased. In that silence pierced by whispers and muffled moans, I had time to meditate on what I'd just been told. Never had I heard those versions of the story. Without my knowing, an entire world of rumors and suspicions had germinated. Everyone seemed to have their own theory.

As I left, I found Garre still leaning against the wall, smoking and conversing with everyone who entered.

"Funerals make things a little livelier," I heard him say in passing. "When there's no one dead or dying, you can't stand how boring it gets."

I nodded goodbye to him.

"Kid," he advised me as I was opening my car door, "if you're going to write about this, please, ask the people who know what they're talking about. Otherwise you won't find out a damn thing."

NICOLÁS ISN'T THERE. They can't find him, you hear on the other side of the window. They're looking for him. He's disappeared. And you still don't know if he was kidnapped, if he's run away, if he's hiding.

That makes you think of hide-and-seek. If Nicolás is hiding, no one will find him. Nobody ever beats him at hide-and-seek. You remember that. His thin body in the irrigation trenches, squeezed into the narrowest pipes, melding into the trees, capable of lifting piles of grass and creeping beneath them like a worm, stretching out, holding his breath, playing dead.

Nicolás knows how to disappear. You, though—they always catch you. Your body doesn't keep pace with you. Your body is a burden, an encumbrance.

All you can manage is to follow Nicolás when you climb the old lemon tree next to the river. He jumps up it and that's that. You use the knots in the broad trunk as footholds. You hold out until the sun sets, facing each other, not uttering a word, just being there, just the two of you. Serene. Immobile. You still don't know if that tranquility will ever return. Or that silence. Or that time congealed.

The afternoon ends with your mother's voice. You're close enough to hear it through the trees. Many years later, when you write a novel to tell this story and you try to recall the moment, it will be easier for you to recover the sonority of your mother's voice than Nicolás's words. Because he never was a voice. He was nothing that ever opened up. He was just a fleeting body. A body that runs and that you never manage to catch.

4

ON MY WAY back from the funeral home, I decided to turn off onto the old road linking Alquerías with the lowlands. In less than two minutes, I was in front of Nicolás's house, and I couldn't help stopping a few seconds to stare at it. Something horrible had occurred there. Inside, where you had played cards so many times. And pachisi. And hide-and-seek. And all the other games children play.

They had repainted the front of the house, and in a corner of the driveway there was now a kind of shed made of sheets of asbestos cement for parking the car. Otherwise, everything was the same. The blue 127 that Nicolás once drove was now a white Fiat Punto. It was probably his dad's car—his dad was the only one who still lived there—and it was parked as meticulously as ever, exactly parallel to the front door, as if someone had lined it up with the aid of a T-square.

Nicolás's house shared a roof with what had once been Julia's. That had been my second home, Julia had been my second mother, but like so many others, she had left the lowlands long ago, and her house was nothing like what it had been. Between those who had moved and those who had died, hardly anyone from my childhood was left. The look of it all had changed too: The former orchards were now overrun by detached houses with gardens and pools. That world no longer belonged to me. The lowlands I had grown up in were starting to disappear.

I write *the lowlands*. Really, I don't know what to call that place I lived in for twenty-five years. La Huerta de Murcia is its name: a kind of natural territory comprising lands irrigated by the Segura River, from the Contraparada—a dam to the city's west that dates back to the Arab times—to the border with Valencia. Every town, every district, has its agricultural area: Torreagüera, Bejaján, Nonduermas...where I grew up, the agricultural zone was known as Los Ramos, about a mile south of the village, in the right bank of the Segura, close to Alquerías, along the old road that links Murcia to Orihuela. There was a village there surrounded by lemon and orange trees, potato fields, rows of lettuce, tomatoes, and other produce of all kinds. Green fields crisscrossed by ditches, canals, and channels that follow plans laid out under Muslim rule and often conserve their Arabic names: Benicomay, Benicoto, Azarbe de Beniel.

The lowlands are a place, but they're also an image, a mythical space. Throughout the nineteenth century, as nationalism reached its peak, the lowlands were synonymous with romantic rootedness and the love for one's soil. An image of authenticity came to surround the life of the inhabitants of Murcia, and a folk culture was born, a way of life, a system of relations, a peculiar body of thought, and even a dialect known as *panocho*. Poets and writers like Vicente Medina helped create that image that still survives today. In a certain way, they invented a tradition.

Nowadays that folk culture has transformed into environmentalism. And the Murcians from the capital who yearn for the authentic life of the lowlanders of the past go out and ride their bikes along the village roads on weekends and gather to protest against real estate speculators, who have more or less destroyed their beloved paradise. Some of these people even build their own houses there with pools, and in their pride at their contact with the genuine, they shout louder than anyone the slogans, "Save the lowlands! Save our traditions! Murcia isn't for sale!"

All my life, I've tried to escape this mythmaking. Life in the lowlands was a purgatory I had to get through to make it to the city. The canals were full of mosquitos. Digging channels through the fields was backbreaking work. There were no lights on the streets, no heat in the houses; we didn't even get the public access channel. In the lowlands, I felt isolated, exiled from the world. I never cared for life among lemon trees, I never felt integrated in the middle of nowhere. Maybe Garre was right. I had never been completely from there.

My three brothers, quite a bit older than I, married and built houses near my parents. Juan and Emilio were on the very same road. José Antonio, the oldest of us, was a mile closer to town, but still surrounded by lemon trees. I was the only one who decided to leave. In 2004, after three years with Raquel, we married. I had met her when I was studying art history, and she and I bought a small apartment in a neighborhood close to town.

Your youngest one's a fancy little city boy, the neighbors told my mother. *He's always looked down on us*, some of them said. And maybe they were right, in part. Because it's true that I had to get out of there. Go far away. It wasn't an easy decision. My father died in 2003, and my mother was left on her own, with just a caretaker who came by to look after her. Thrombosis had taken her mobility along with a great deal of her lucidity. I was the youngest, and it was my duty to step in. My wife would have to understand. That was part of the deal. You marry someone and you take whatever comes with it. That was how things were in the lowlands. And that was how it was supposed to have been.

I'm aware that more than one person still can't grasp how I did what I did, how I could abandon my mother and go live close to the city. *Young people don't respect nothing no more. It's over. Respect, tradition, the past. That's done. All people want now is their own house, to live far away. The fewer obligations, the better. There's no respect for anything anymore.* My ears would ring when I heard that. And it's not as if anyone ever dared to say it to my face. But I knew they were thinking it, that they were murmuring it amongst themselves. *So, you made it out, huh? You're going to ruin the few years of life your mother has left.*

I had to be selfish and live my own life. That place, not just the lowlands but that house that had slowly gathered diseases inside it—first Nena's, then my father's, then my mother's—sucked up all my energy. Leaving for the university every morning was a breath of fresh air. Going back was a prison sentence. I don't understand how I ever managed to write anything in that dense, somber house. Eventually, not even the bunker I had built for myself in one corner of the yard to try to read and write was sufficient.

I wanted out. I wanted far away from my family. I couldn't take the constant questions from my cousins and sisters-in-law. *Where are you off to so late? Nice car you got there. You've got money to go out to fancy dinners, but not enough to buy Christmas presents for your nieces and nephews.* I couldn't stand being supervised. I spent my entire childhood and adolescence in the domestic panopticon, and now I wanted to live with my wife somewhere no one could control me. I didn't care where. I just wanted to get away. Luckily, Raquel had the same feeling. And her experience was similar too. Get out of the lowlands, away from the surveillance of our neighbors, go somewhere where you didn't have to say hi to your downstairs neighbor, where people wouldn't enter your home without asking, where nobody kept track of what you were buying, what you did, how you dressed, what time you left, what time you got home. Where you could live as you liked. That's what I wanted. That is still the greatest thing I've ever achieved. Building my impenetrable fortress. A home, hermetic, where nobody can enter uninvited.

The lowlands were in the past. Especially after my mother's death. My brothers still lived there, my cousins, my nieces and nephews. The house I'd inherited was still there, though it would soon fall apart. My childhood was there, it's true. But I didn't want to go live there again. Not in that house, not on that road. And yet, every time I visited my brothers and looked at my old home from a distance, every time I passed down the road through that village in my car, I felt the prick of nostalgia. A contradictory nostalgia. Because a person feels nostalgia for the things they want back: the pain of distance, a longing to repossess. The one thing I knew for certain in that moment was that I never wanted to return there. And yet something shifted inside me every time I entered the lowlands. Where did that feeling come from? Was it my origins, calling out to me? Was it the cry of a land I never knew how to hear?

The afternoon I came back from the funeral home and stopped a few seconds in front of my friend's house, I felt that paradoxical nostalgia returning to me. In that place, the darkest, most terrible thing had happened. And yet, that space was an origin. An origin that exerted an inexplicable power over me. Attraction and refraction. A diagonal force that pulled me downward and at the same time pushed me away. A strange energy that threatened to shatter me.

TAKE CARE OF my Nicolás.

His mother says this on the first day of school. You remember that. It's the first notion of him you possess. A phrase. In line at school. The first day, next to each other.

You're both crying. No one wants to be left alone. You hear his mother's words. You see Nicolás's hand grasping his mother's dress tight.

Take care of my Nicolás, she says again.

And you stop crying then and you grab his hand. Nicolás's hand.

Her words are a foundation. The beginning of a routine. You will try to do this from that day forward. You feel this responsibility. Take care of Nicolás. Be his protector, his armor, his shell when faced with the world.

Miguel Ángel is Nicolás's skin, your teacher, María Ángeles, will tell your mother years later. She'll repeat this any time the subject of your friendship comes up, praising your sense of duty, your commitment to that friendship.

Nicolás's skin.

It was that way on the first day of preschool, it stayed that way in junior high, in Sunday school, during your time as altar boys. Even later, when you were in driver's ed, and he learned to steer that car that is no longer in the driveway.

Nicolás's skin, you think. Skin. Nothing else. Because you've never really known what lay beneath that epidermis. You were skin. Armor. A door, but one you were never able to open. You didn't get inside, and maybe that's why now you understand nothing and you feel helpless. Like a serpent's empty skin. The inert vestige of a body that's now gone elsewhere.

5

THE CONVERSATION WITH Garre and my sister-in-law and that moment observing my friend's house opened the floodgates violently to the past. I needed to finish the novel I was working on, *The Instant of Danger*, and the memory of that time was taking up too much space in my mind. I wanted to slough it off, push it aside, but no matter where I went or what I did, it insisted stubbornly on remaining there. On every visit to the lowlands, in every conversation with my brother Juan at the stadium as we watched Real Murcia lose another match, every time I saw my nieces and nephews... above all, it began to appear on Saturday mornings, when I would have lunch with my brothers at El Yeguas, a tavern in the lowlands along one of the roads that lead to the village of Los Ramos.

El Yeguas had been my father's second home. My mother used to call there to notify him that lunch was ready or dinner was on the table getting cold. When he died, the biggest wreath on his coffin wasn't from his children, his wife, or his grandchildren, it was the one that said *In Loving Memory, El Yeguas Tavern.*

The owners of the bar—the sons of old man Yeguas, who reopened their father's place in the nineties—are like family to us. On one wall of the dining room, framed like a painting, is a newspaper clipping about me. *Writing a book about my parents' death saved my life*, the headline reads. Proudly, my brothers usually sit near that photo. And it is near that photo where the four of us meet, at least once every two months, to eat together and catch up. We call it lunch, but for me, it's usually breakfast. At ten in the morning, they've already been up for half the day and have no problem putting away blood sausages, bacon, grilled beef, and a few glasses of wine. I've just pulled myself out of bed, and all that mingles badly in my stomach with my coffee with milk and the toast I haven't yet begun to digest.

I enter with my eyes still swollen after a sleepless night, and the racket inside startles me. On the other side of the aluminum door, behind the blinds, it seems I've journeyed into the past. As in those Parisian arcades that inspired Walter Benjamin's effusive reflections, in El Yeguas, there persists the throbbing of a world that began to die out some time ago—the agonies of a way of life that will never return. There I find the tractor driver, the field hand who grafts the lemon trees, the soil fumigator, the man who decides in what order to irrigate, the security guard, the bricklayer who built the garages, the guy who sells lottery tickets, the Korean, Fao, Nenico, Pepele, Litri, Churrispas...with all those faces who populate my memories of childhood. They're still there, most of them retired now, a few others on the dole, drinking muscat-and-anisette and playing dominos and cards, sending each other videos on WhatsApp and uploading photos of the village fair to Facebook. El Yeguas is a door to the past, a vestige of the lowlands of before, but it has Wi-Fi now, and Movistar Plus so people can watch the soccer games from Madrid.

Ever since I began to consider the possibility of writing this book, these lunches at El Yeguas have changed. Going back there means not only seeing my brothers again after our parents' death; it's also come to mean literature, that universe I've always thought was so distant from my origins. As I wrote or thought about this story, I felt my two worlds coming together. And I saw that this was true the day my brother Emilio let drop at the bar that I wanted to write a story about the murder at Rosario's home. Until then, nobody who went to El Yeguas for lunch every day had cared about anything I'd written. Despite the press clippings on the walls, no one knew much about those books I'd published about art and aesthetics. But the mere mention of the murder at Rosario's home brought the locals over to our table. I was going to write something that had touched all of them. And for the first time, what I did, my job, seemed to have some meaning.

This came up the first time at the end of our meal, over a bottle of herb liquor and angel hair pastries. I opened the Notes app on my phone and wrote down everything, as if the true process of documentation for the novel had begun in that moment. I still didn't know if I would do any proper interviews; I had no idea how I'd use this conversation, or even if it would serve any purpose.

Everyone seemed to have something to say. And everyone wanted to say it.

"The Cain of Murcia. I remember perfectly, that was what the headlines called him."

"It was awful. The worst thing that ever happened around here."

"Like the Puerto Hurraco massacre."

"There was something going on between the two of them. The parents knew it too."

"He was a pervert, same as the rest of the family. They were just weird. You could tell when you looked in their eyes."

"There's a lot more to that story."

A lot more to that story. And it hadn't been forgotten. Nothing was resolved, and the theories and speculation had gone on growing over time. I was familiar with these conjectures—they were the same ones I'd heard from Garre. Everyone spoke, but not many had much to say.

One of the bar's owners, Antolín, the younger of the two brothers, wanted to have his say too: "I saw him that morning. I'd gotten up and I saw him speeding past at three-thirty. He didn't even wave."

Antolín sounded wounded. He used to play soccer with us in the park and in the chard fields. He might have been the last person to see Nicolás alive. One thing was sure: Antolín wasn't just talking to hear his own voice. So Nicolás had taken that road to El Cabezo instead of the one that passed through Alquerías. I didn't know this then, but later this apparently irrelevant information would prove useful. For now, I just noted it down.

I noted down what my brother Juan said as well. Juan, who always waited for others to finish so he could have the last word. He had gone into the house with my father that night and had seen everything.

"I saw it, what happened. There was blood everywhere. All over. I remember that. Spots of blood on the ceiling even."

"How'd you get in?" I asked.

"Dad and me, we just burst in, we didn't ask. We stuck around till the Civil Guard kicked us out. I remember Rosi was lying on the ground. Jesus . . . I won't forget that sight for the rest of my life. The blood . . . I'm talking blood everywhere."

"He killed her with the tape player," Antolín butted in. "That's what they say."

"I'm not sure," Juan replied, "but the tape player *was* destroyed. And the blood, it was on the sheets, on the curtains, even on the lamp. I've never seen that kind of blood."

"The coroner's report must say what happened," my brother Emilio said.

This gave way to more speculation:

"He blew a fuse."

"It was a long time coming."

"You can say that again."

"He had a screw loose."

"For sure."

"There's something there we don't know."

"The report," Emilio repeated. "It's all got to be in there."

"I guess," I said. "But I don't think it will be easy to get hold of."

"I used to know one of the officers on the case," Juan intervened. "The one who told us to leave the room. But I lost contact with him."

"If he can't help," Antolín said, pointing to one corner of the bar, "there's always Abellán."

Abellán used to work for the National Police. The Civil Guard had carried out the investigation, but he'd been close to the case. He lived in the lowlands; there was no way he could just stay clear of it. Now he was a reserve deputy, and he spent his dead hours playing cards in El Yeguas. He'd been sitting there self-absorbed for a long time that morning, but he'd glanced over more than once, and he must have been paying attention to our conversation. This suspicion was confirmed when he heard his name and reacted, clutching his bottle of beer:

"All that's over and done with. There's no mystery there. It's over. Now please . . ." At this he turned to me. "Be a good boy and don't go stirring up shit."

ARE YOU HUNGRY? Julia asks.

You nod. You're always hungry, even now.

She walks over to the bench where you're sitting and lifts the tea towel covering the Christmas sweets. Nougat, almond cookies, candied fruits, shortbread, pastries with powdered sugar like snow. You don't know which to choose, so you take one of each, laying them on a napkin and eating them one at a time.

Food calms everything. Outside is tragedy, inside are Julia's desserts.

She's always bought sweets for you, ever since you were a little boy. Every afternoon, there was always some prefab sweet, chocolate cake with cream filling, pastry with cacao, chocolate cupcakes, Nocilla sandwiches. More than half of your two hundred twenty pounds are Julia's sweets.

You used to share them with Nicolás. But he never got fat, no matter what he ate. His body was always wiry. Fatty and Skinny, people used to joke. At school, at soccer practice, and even later, in town, in catechism, preparing for confirmation. Fatty and Skinny. Not a single girl ever looked at you. Nicolás didn't mind, or that's what you thought. It shattered you inside, though.

Fatty and Skinny. It was the same on field trips. For the kids from your school and the kids from the other school that traveled along with you.

But then one night, some girls spoke to you. They asked you what your name was and sat at your table. You didn't know how to act. You were timid. As much as Nicolás, maybe more.

The next day, you had breakfast at the girls' table. That's the closest you ever came to hooking up. You remember the mischievous look in Nicolás's eyes. You don't know which of you was more nervous.

At lunch, they sat on the other end of the table. That was it, nothing had happened. But it didn't matter. That's one of your happiest memories. And Nicolás is a part of it.

6

THE LAST SUNDAY in May and the first Saturday in June is the town fair in Los Ramos, held in honor of Our Lady of the Lowlands. It is our biggest celebration. That Sunday afternoon, the members of the Brotherhood of the Virgin carry her on her throne to the village church, where she remains until the following Saturday, when they take her back in a procession to the chapel.

Ever since I left, my oldest brother has invited me back every year for the fair, and for the Saturday evening dinner at the park in front of the chapel. We'll hold your place, he tells me, just in case. I always find the perfect excuse not to go. Sometimes I really can't—I'm traveling, or I have a lecture to give—but most of the time, I don't feel like it. I've already had my fair share of processions. As a teenager, I guided the faithful of the Brotherhood, carried the Virgin, helped prepare her throne, tolled the bells, even played hymns and songs of praise to Our Lady on the organ. I remember those days clearly: the Brotherhood's endless meetings the week before we took her up and brought her down, the arguments, the reproaches about who was a shirker and who had to pick up the slack, the moments of tension along the way, the interminable Mass in the village church, the pain in my feet, the inflammation in my shoulder the next day, how uncomfortable my folk costume was, how absurd it looked on my misshapen body, and especially, the anxious sensation of being the center of all eyes in the village for a few hours. I don't miss any of that. I never felt the least devotion that might give meaning to those events. Deep down, it was just an obligation, a commitment I didn't know how to wriggle out of. For my brother, though, it remains the most important moment of the year. In a sense, he lived for it. It's not so much about devotion—though there's some of that too—it's affection. Because he's the one who carved the Virgin, designed the chapel, and initiated the procession. All that when he was little more than a teenager.

At the beginning of this novel I wrote that there were no books in my house and I was the first one to bring them home to fill the shelves. What I didn't mention was that this same house was full of sculptures of clay and plaster and that my oldest brother is a sculptor. The other two, Juan and Emilio, quit school early and went to work with my father at the aluminum factory. They helped out in the fields, went out with him to plant and sow, cleared the irrigation canals, burnt the brush after weeding. José Antonio never wanted to do any of that. Since he was little, he'd go down by the canals, set aside his hoe and sickle, and entertain himself making figures out of mud. That was the origin of his first Christ, his first Virgin, his first saints. My parents always told it that way, like a chapter in the family's mythology: the artist who emerged from the fields.

I owe to him much of what I am. That includes my name. He was the one who dissuaded my parents from calling me Cristóbal, in memory of the Francoist grandfather I might write a novel about one day, and convinced them to call me Miguel Ángel, after his favorite sculptor, the great Michelangelo Buonarroti. José Antonio was my godfather, after all. It was only right that he have some say in the matter.

I preserve hardly any memories of him from my childhood. He married early and moved out of my parents' house before I turned five, and everything before then is hazy. What I do remember clearly is the astonishment and fear I felt the first time I found myself surrounded by the sculptures piled up on the shelves, as though displayed in a chamber of curiosities. These clay and plaster figurines were models for his first wood carvings, and still bore marks from the pencil my brother used to transfer the image from one medium to another. I still sense that visual landscape, that gallery of faces, torsos, and dismembered bodies burned on my retina, persisting in my way of viewing the world.

That disconcerting domestic museum conserved only a part of my brother's sculptures, the ones that had survived the passage of time and our family's iconoclasm. In the past, my mother's father—my communist grandfather—used to toss my brother Emilio a bit of spare change to climb up there and destroy the saints and throw the pieces of them out the window. That was his way of taking vengeance on those who had locked him up at the end of the Civil War because they heard him say when the minor basilica in Elche caught fire, *Look how she burns, the Virgin Mary, glory be unto her.* My mother told me that later, regretting how she'd been party to that destruction in the years when she'd tried to convince my brother to take an administrative position at the credit union.

Fortunately, the iconoclasm failed, and today, José Antonio is one of the most respected sculptors of icons in Spain. In a way, it was thanks to his influence that I opted to study art history. I had a clear idea of what art was: his religious sculptures. Then everything changed, and I found myself writing about urinals turned upside down, invisible paintings, extreme performances—the art that interests me today. But, as an art historian, there are things I can still admit, and one of them is that my brother is good at what he does. Quite a bit better than I am at what I do.

If I can't keep myself from writing these paragraphs now, I suppose it's from pure admiration—an admiration it's often hard for me to show. And because I believe he opened a path that I was able to walk down later, in my own way. He stayed and I left, he's an acclaimed artist, and in the village and the lowlands people still refer to me as *the sculptor's brother.* A sculptor who invited me to the procession the year I'd decided my book would be about my friend the murderer, as he had done every year since I left. We'll hold a place for you, he repeated. And for the first time in many years, I didn't give my usual response, I said yes, he could count on me, I'd be there watching his Virgin as she arrived at the chapel amid acclaim. Obviously I wasn't interested in gawking at the floral arrangements on the throne or the new painting on the standard or the dexterity of the throne bearers or their emotion as they sang the national anthem. I agreed for a different reason: because I was certain that attending would help with what I wanted to write. It might be a way of returning to the past, which, unconsciously or maybe not so unconsciously, I wanted to awaken, make denser, more palpable, feeling that it was still there, frozen in time, waiting for me.

For more than half an hour, Raquel and I waited for the Virgin without a moment to ourselves. One after another, neighbors and acquaintances passed and greeted me:

"Hey, it's been ages."

"I thought you'd disappeared."

"Where have you been? We haven't seen hide nor hair from you."

"Bet you forgot about all this, right?"

"The prodigal son returns..."

Everything sounded like a reproach, and I justified myself as best I could: I've been busy, work, you know, plus my travel dates always clash, I'm basically never home, but yeah, I really do need to stop by more often...

I could sense that none of these excuses was satisfactory. Nor were my evasions of such indiscreet questions as:

"Is this your wife? I used to know your husband when he was just this high, before he got all big and fat."

"When are the kids coming? You two are going to fool around and miss the boat."

"You'll baptize them in the chapel, right? The photos afterward are so nice, with the Virgin in the background."

"How are things in the capital? It's a shame your mother's house is going to wind up falling into the ground. When are you going to fix it up and come back where you belong?"

A kind of déjà vu, all of it. And this was what I had run away from. The scrutiny, the pressure of gossip, people's presumption that they had a right to ask about your life and tell you how to run it, that need to constantly justify every little thing you did. Now, as I write this and glance at my Instagram and Twitter, I know I haven't made it all the way out, that I'm still being watched, that I still have to explain why I'm going where I'm going, why I'm having dinner in such-and-such a place, my readings, my actions... the surveillance system has become far more extreme. The only difference is that now I'm purposely exposing myself to others. They don't have to ask anymore. I'm my own sentry.

This is what I'm thinking today, but that afternoon my neighbors' questions and comments forced me to relive the feeling of being watched as a teenager. And they kept me from thinking tranquilly of that past I was trying to call up. I had gone there like a flaneur in time, a pedestrian of memory, trying to drag the past into the present in silence, in slow motion. But the past appeared not as a fixed image, but rather as motile, a murmuring. I never found a moment to sneak into the chapel, the place where I'd thought I could find Nicolás's presence and steep myself in my recollections of him. And that is why I'd gone there. To rouse his ghost. This was the place our childhood had occurred. On Sundays, as altar boys, and later, in our teenage years, when we were preparing the readings for Mass. In front of that same door we had spent dead afternoons sitting on benches, playing cards under the shadows of the trees, using oranges for basketballs and trash cans for nets, guessing which car would pass on the road by its sound and speed.

That afternoon, I could evoke none of that—not in the placid way I do now as I write. And yet, Nicolás's memory appeared in a way I hadn't predicted. At least not until I saw the Virgin's throne approaching up the road. In that moment, I knew what was about to happen.

During the village fair the year after Nicolás killed his sister, I was still a member of the Brotherhood. I had entered four years before, just when I started high school. I was a kid, but I was big and burly and could carry the Virgin without any difficulty. There were fifteen of us, and that year we met, as usual, a few weeks before the procession to prepare the throne and plan the festivities.

Those gatherings were always tense. All the reproaches from the year before came to light—who walked out of step, who showed up late, who couldn't find their folk costume and instead put on whatever shirt they could find. . . . But in 1996, everything was calm. We convened in the city hall in Los Ramos, no one upbraided anyone, and we finished earlier than planned.

I remember it clearly, especially when Nicolás's older brother walked in and everyone fell silent. He sat at a corner of the meeting table and didn't open his mouth the entire time.

I hadn't seen him since his brother and sister were buried. I hadn't had the courage then to give my condolences, not to him, not to his parents, not to his other brother who was still alive. But now, I thought now was a good time to do so.

I spent the entire meeting asking myself about what I should say to him when it was over. I wanted him to see that it had hurt me too, maybe almost as much as it had him, that Nicolás was my friend, that I had suffered. Phrases crossed through my mind, harsh, profound, that would show how near his pain was to mine. But I soon realized everything I could say would tell only half the story, and that in his mind, everything must be quite different. Nicolás was a part of it, of course, he was his little brother, but he was also the man who had killed his sister, his Rosi. What hurt most for him? Losing a brother? Losing a sister? His brother being the killer who had ended his sister's life?

I think that was the first time I put myself in his shoes and tried to understand the battle that must have been going on inside him, his contradictory and irreconcilable sentiments about what had occurred. And maybe that was why, when we were done and I gathered the courage to approach him, all I managed to say was, "I'm really sorry."

"Thanks," he replied.

His expression didn't change, almost as if I hadn't spoken. Only for an instant did I perceive in his eyes the beginnings of tears that didn't flow. It was brief, maybe less than a second. A breakdown that didn't occur. Then everything went back to normal. He pulled himself together, turned, and talked to the other members of the Brotherhood.

I couldn't understand it, that strange feeling of normality, as though nothing had happened at all. I guess I imagined he'd be destroyed, his face gaunt with suffering, his eyes swollen from so much crying. I had even imagined he wouldn't show up to the gathering that year, that he wouldn't dress in his folk costume and help bring out the Virgin, that he'd stay away from the fair, and especially from the dinner in the park and the dance afterward. But there he was, as if everything was the same as always, as if nothing hurt, as if his brother—my friend—hadn't killed his sister and hadn't thrown himself off a cliff.

Afterward, I didn't speak to him again—or anyone else from the Brotherhood, really—but every time I saw him over the years, I struggled not to think of Nicolás.

He was living proof that the nightmare had really occurred. And year after year, shocked by his unalterably normal expression, I couldn't stop wondering about his pain, how time might lessen it, mitigate it, make it eventually disappear. But this was all speculation, because his face never revealed anything. It remained a border, an unbreachable wall.

That same indecipherable expression was the one I saw that afternoon when I attended the procession, hoping to make palpable the story I wished to tell. At first, he didn't see me, apparently concentrated on bearing the throne on his left shoulder. I had time to look at him closely. Unlike the other members of the Brotherhood, he hadn't gotten fatter or lost his hair, which was dark and lustrous, like his brother's. He seemed to have gotten stuck in time. He must have been the same age as my brothers, well into his fifties, but he didn't look much older than forty. And that made everything seem all the more sinister. When, moments before the Virgin entered the chapel, our eyes met, I saw on his face the same expression as on that afternoon when I'd dared to say, "I'm sorry."

He nodded, and we held each other's stare. I don't know if seeing me after so long—seeing his brother's best friend—called forth the past for him the same way it did for me. No one would have known from just looking at him. Nor could he have known from looking at me what was passing through my mind. And of course, he could never have imagined that a primordial part of his story was taking shape within me, that what he seemed to have buried behind the appearance of normalcy was now being dug up, and I was attempting to revive it. Twenty years later.

That reencounter made me aware that the past isn't just a memory, immaterial, an intangible mental projection. The past is dense, it breathes, it moves among us. I went there to recall it, as if it were an inert and manipulable object, and it looked me straight in the eyes, totally alive and totally dead.

I couldn't rid myself of that feeling all afternoon, not even later, when I was having dinner with my family in the park and paying little attention to the stories my brothers told about my nieces and nephews. I couldn't stop glancing over at the table where Nicolás's brother was sitting. How normal he was acting, conversing with his wife, joking around, enjoying the evening as if he were just another guy, as if the past hadn't destroyed him forever. That was when I sensed for the first time that in that exceptional normalcy, which I had found so strange, there was a kind of real normalcy—that the walls a person raises to isolate himself from pain sometimes serve their purpose.

I think that was the night when I decided I'd never try to talk to him about what Nicolás did. That I wouldn't dig into the wound or try to knock down the wall. And I asked myself if I could write about his past while at the same time respecting his pain. I didn't find an answer. Even today, I still haven't.

DON'T GO, SON. Don't leave me alone.

I'm sorry, Julia. I have to.

You can't stand it inside. You can't remain there, hiding, like her. You're not a child. Not anymore.

The sun still hasn't risen. The driveway is still full of neighbors and Civil Guards. It looks more like a movie than anything you've ever seen. Like a horror film.

You try to pick up on what the agents are saying, but you can't make out a single word. They go inside. Through the front and back doors.

A few seconds later, your brother comes out, and everyone mills around him.

What happened, Juan? What did you see? How was she killed? Where?

She was bludgeoned, he replies. In her room. There's blood everywhere. Even on the ceiling.

You think of the house. Its interior. You've gone in there thousands of times. But never into that room.

That door was always shut.

The kitchen. The living room. The door in the back. The same door that's been there as long as you can remember. That door is your first memory of that house.

Even before you saw Nicolás lining up for school, you saw that door. The closed door, visible from where the telephone sits.

Rosario's phone. The only one around. The phone your mother used to call from. She'd call your uncle in Almeria, your aunts and uncles in Elche, even your family in Argentina. And of course, your brother Juan, for those twenty months when he was doing his military service in the Canary Islands.

In your memory, you might be three years old. Your mother is sitting in a wicker chair and you are on her lap. You've just been handed the receiver of the green telephone hanging on the wall.

On the other line, you hear your brother's voice.

Don't say anything, your mother warns you.

Your head is bandaged. You want to tell him about the accident. Your cousin, a loaded shotgun, an explosion that nearly cost you your life.

Juanito, you say, I got shot. My head's all bandaged. I look like the Indian kid from that Japanese show about the bears.

Playing. Heroism. And in the depths of that memory, the door. A closed door. Rosi's room. An invisible stage. A stage set for the horror.

7

TWO WEEKS OR so after I attended the procession, I finished the final draft of my novel *The Instant of Danger*, just in time to send it to the Herralde Prize. It would make the shortlist. I finished my classes and graded my exams and finally was able to breathe. Not for long, though. In less than a month, my life would change completely. I had received a grant from Cornell University to research the use of time in contemporary art and was going to spend the next academic year on the other side of the ocean. In Ithaca, New York, I'd have to put fiction aside and return to the essay until my stay was over. I'd gotten the grant as an art historian, not as a novelist. And so the book that I had in my head would have to wait until I returned to Spain.

And yet, in the month I had left before flying to the United States, I began to seriously plan the new novel. I didn't care that in a few weeks, everything would come to a halt: I laid out what might be the structure and thought of the possible sources I would turn to for information about my subject.

The event had made an impact, and news of it appeared in all the media. I needed to know what the reporters had said, how they had treated the case. It wouldn't be hard to find the newspapers from those days. I would also try to find the TV news reports. I would see my own testimony before the camera: would know what I said that day, would see myself twenty years later. Harder to get hold of would be the judicial and forensic reports. But I didn't yet know how hard.

By the time I found out, June was nearly over. I had spent the time drawing up plans, tracing out possibilities. Only at the end, with just a week left before leaving, did I try to find information I could take with me to Ithaca.

On the websites of the national papers, there wasn't a single word about it, not on the 26th, the 27th, or the 28th of December of 1995. The local papers that had reported on the case, *La Verdad* and *La Opinión*, hadn't begun publishing their online edition until 2006 and 2008. On the webpages of the TV and radio stations, I didn't find anything either.

The world of the past lay beyond the internet. It was curious to see the lack of search results when I googled for "the Cain of Murcia" or the names of Nicolás or his sister. I imagined a historian in the future whose only source of information was the internet. We often say you can find everything there, but there is an entire world, a real world, that exists beyond it. If this murder had happened ten years later, I thought, there would be news of it everywhere, ghostly residues of information floating in cyberspace waiting for someone to notice, and social media would be rife with comments and speculation.

But no: That was a past that didn't belong to this world, one situated in a kind of prehistory, a history before the information era. I couldn't help but think how all that would disappear forever along with the witnesses, never taking up residence in the digital realm. But if I wrote something, if I spoke of the crime in an interview, if my book was digitized and downloaded legally or pirated, I would make that past present, situating in the computerized display case where we live an event that perhaps ought to remain hidden forever.

I considered all this as I surfed around the net without finding any results. I needed to move beyond the screen, to the physical world I'd almost forgotten how to move in, as I realized when, the week before leaving for Ithaca, I walked into the library of the School of Arts and Letters, assuming they still kept a periodical archive. When I asked, the librarians looked at me with surprise. I hadn't put in any requests there for ten years, and I didn't know the archive now had a building of its own on campus.

When I found it and asked where I could consult the old newspapers, once again, I had to lower my head in embarrassment as I was told:

"We don't keep those here. Just academic journals."

I left feeling asphyxiated, as if I'd entered a foreign country, and I wondered what I was doing.

I had to go to the city's archives, assuming they still existed. They must have held on to the local papers. I could have gone there the next day, but I decided I'd do it when I was back in the country. It didn't make much sense, hurrying over, making all those copies, and taking the whole pile of them on my trip. I would need time to go through everything carefully. Not only find the reports, but also consider what else was happening at that time. Look at the film section, see what the new releases were, all the movies I didn't go see, all I lost that Christmas season because I was in mourning, the soccer scores, the classifieds, the week's news. That would take days, and I didn't have them just then.

And to consult the archives of Spanish National Television in Murcia, I needed something more than time. I called every number I could find for them on the internet: the regional director of programming, the news director, the archivist. None of it got me anywhere. What I wanted was apparently too difficult to obtain. Many of the archives had been moved. And nobody was inclined to go to great lengths to find those recordings simply because I'd asked for them.

And so I gave up. That was the first time I'd do so—the first of many. I gave up, and I felt relieved. In essence, I had found what I was looking for. The university archive no longer had the newspapers I needed, the television station refused to help me find the video, and that was freeing. It meant I could leave in peace. In relative peace.

THE BROTHERS ARRIVE. Two in the same car. They park in front of the house. They lay claim to their space. People stand aside. There's silence in the driveway. Everyone observes the scene. They get out and hug their father.

My Rosi, my Nicolás . . . , the father says.

Hush, they whisper, don't say more.

Everything is audible. Everything echoes.

Fireworks break the silence. It's seven in the morning. They're celebrating Christmas the next village over. Today the Savior is born, the Messiah, the Lord.

You see the paradox. Nicolás rises up in your mind. You remember him crouching, fingers in his ears, face covered, terrified, as if the world were coming to an end. And running, disappearing, saying nothing to anyone, fleeing the racket, the opening volley in a war.

Him crying. Him running. Him escaping. And everyone celebrating. Firecrackers at the village fair, a castle made of fireworks, bottle rockets for newlyweds, for newborns, for Christ resurrected.

You don't know where Nicolás is, but you suppose that when he heard the explosion, he took off running, trying to escape the noise, looking for the cave where he'll feel protected, the corner, the balustrade, the bed, the sofa . . . a refuge from the storm. And now, you think, this explosion is the thing that matters least. The crackling of the bottle rockets. Because now, the noise is inside his head, not out—the roar, the explosion, the bellowing of thunder. Piercing his brain, perhaps, and stirring him up inside.

8

I SAID GOODBYE to everyone as if I were traveling to Ithaca forever: to my closest friends, and to the friends I hadn't seen in a long time. I wanted to say something to Juan Alberto, Nicolás's cousin, as well—the same cousin I had been putting off ever since the afternoon when I found him after Sergio del Molino presented his latest book.

The last Friday of July, two days before I left for the United States, we managed to meet at a bar close to the university. I had to get a few books from my office, and I asked if that afternoon would work. I got hung up, and I texted him to let him know I'd be late. When I arrived, he was outside the bar, walking nervously among the empty tables on the patio. That struck me as normal. There are people you associate with certain postures, and Juan Alberto wasn't somebody I imagined sitting down. In my mind, he was always standing, walking, running, exercising, moving forward.

We hugged, and we sat outside. It was hot, but the temperature was tolerable with a beer, which I ordered as soon as I had settled into my chair.

"Beer, Miguel?" he asked. "My, how you've changed."

It had been more than fifteen years since we'd last met for a drink, and many things had changed. In the old days, I always drank Diet Coke, and I barely ever touched alcohol. My life was like that of the protagonist of my first novel, a timid, anxious student who preferred to stay home and read while everyone else went out to the bars. There was still something of that person inside me, but I had gotten over some of my hang-ups, and I went out often—usually at night—trying to make up for lost time.

And that was what we tried to do over several hours that evening. As he'd mentioned, he now had shared custody of his daughter. That was the most important event in his life in the past few years. He showed me some photos of her on his phone. He said little about work as a policeman, about climbing the ranks, or about the girl he was going out with. He had his daughter back, and that was all that seemed to matter.

As he spoke, I looked at his close-cropped blond hair and his trim goatee. Try as I might, I couldn't imagine him as a father. He was still my friend from my teenage years, the most responsible one, the most adult. He's mature beyond his years, my parents used to say, and it was true. I wanted to be like him. Resolute, open, good-natured, brave. And I'll admit it, I wanted his looks. I envied them above all else. *The German*, people used to call him. Not just because he was born in Germany—his parents, like so many others in Spain, had emigrated in the seventies—but because he was tall and blond with blue eyes. On our field trip to Andorra, he was the only one who managed to kiss a girl. When he got back on the bus, we all applauded.

We were inseparable all through high school. Then the end came, and we drifted apart. I started college, and a little later, he attended police academy. And we lost contact. Our lives took their own directions. But he had always been there. Any time something important has happened in my life, he's always been there, the first to offer to lend a hand. On my wedding day, he was one of the groomsmen. After the ceremony, I hugged him and burst into tears.

The closeness between us isn't something I can explain. It's just the kind of friendship you have with someone you've known since childhood. There's something that stays there forever, an affinity, a fraternal love that never dies, and every time we see each other again, it's reborn.

"I keep track of you in the papers," he said, grabbing a copy of *20 Minutos* that had been lying on the table. He flipped through it and added, "I'm reading the news sometimes and all of a sudden I'm like, *Oh shit, it's Miguel. He's taking off.*"

I smiled. He was up to date on everything in my life. He said he saw my brothers on the road sometimes and asked them about me. He knew I'd written a novel too, but he hadn't read it.

"So, going off to make your fortune in America, no? Where, exactly?"

"Ithaca. Like Ulysses."

I told him Ithaca was a town not far from New York City and that I would be there for a year.

"If I can get some time off and find a cheap ticket, I'll come see you for a week."

"You should," I told him. "We'll have a blast."

In that moment, I knew I was lying. Or being less than sincere. What was I going to talk to him about for a whole week? We had already caught up, and now there was nothing else to say. It was true there was a special closeness between us. We would do anything for each other. But the very different directions our lives had taken meant that, after bringing each other up to date, all we could do was talk about our school days. That was what we had in common, and without it, we were strangers. We couldn't talk about movies, books, or music. We belonged to two separate worlds.

We spent the afternoon talking about our mischief at school; about how I was the only one of our group of four who hadn't become a cop—Juan Alberto was with the National Police, Carlos with the local force, and Fran with the Civil Guard; about how they had hidden in the closet in Latin class and had pretended to be clothes hanging there when the teacher found them; about the time Juan Alberto hit me in the face with a ball in gym class; about how he hid my textbook the day before an exam and I almost got the first F of my life. We talked about everything and nothing: elementary school, high school, our antics in the fields, my failed attempt to ride my bike to El Cabezo de la Plata, our endless games of *Contra* on the Nintendo. The one thing we didn't talk about, even once, was Nicolás.

We never had since that fateful evening. If Nicolás showed up in our conversations, it was always looking back nostalgically at some moment without mentioning what had happened afterward: *Remember that time we jerked down my cousin's pants?* Or: *He was a fast fucker, it was impossible to get the ball out of his hands.* We didn't talk about what he'd seen that night. It was like a blind spot in our conversation. I had never dared to ask him how he'd found the corpse in the gully, what the search had been like, how he had felt afterward. It was as if all that had never happened.

But that evening, I was ready to change that. I'd agreed to meet to say goodbye—to say goodbye because I was leaving for a year when we hadn't seen each other for ten?—but what I really wanted, all I wanted, was to talk to him about the book I was planning. In a way, I wanted his approval.

We had put away a few beers, and I still hadn't figured out a way to bring the issue up. More than two hours had passed, and I was afraid Juan Alberto would soon get up and leave.

"Should we finish off with a gin-and-tonic?" I asked him. "I've got something I want to tell you."

"You're going for the strong stuff. Sure, I'm in."

I got up and ordered at the bar. While they were mixing our drinks and dropping them off, I walked to the bathroom, took a breath, and found the words I wanted:

"I'm going to write a book about what happened," I blurted out when I was back outside.

"What?"

"About Nicolás," I clarified. "About that night."

Juan Alberto lifted his glass, took a small sip, and stared at me briefly, unsure how to react. I didn't know if he was surprised or uncomfortable.

"But I'll be kind," I added to break the silence. "To him, I mean."

"You have to," he finally said. "He was our friend. And that will always be true."

"Yeah," I responded. "He'll always be our friend. That's what I think too."

I told him that would be the thesis of the book, my motive for writing it: that despite what he had allegedly done, it was hard for me to imagine him differently, and my relationship with him couldn't change. He would always be the same companion he'd been.

I fleshed out this notion as I spoke, not sure if it was true or a lie. Later, it struck me that this was actually the idea that interested me: the impossibility of changing our perspective on things, the awareness that there are feelings that others can never replace.

Apart from telling him about my project, I'd wanted to ask him what had happened that night, what he saw, what he'd managed to find out later. I also wanted to know if he'd learned anything else after becoming a policeman, if he'd investigated, if he'd taken any interest in the case at all. I'd even considered asking if he could help me find the case files. But I'd lacked the courage to keep pressing him. The way Juan Alberto had uttered the words *he was our friend* seemed to seal off that possibility. His response, his gaze, was closed off rather than open. That part of him remained blocked, and there was no getting inside, not then, at least.

"I hope you'll let me know when you publish it," he said. "That's something I'll actually read."

"You'll be in it," I said jokingly.

He smiled. "Then make me strong and handsome. And give me a bunch of girlfriends."

MY ROSI, MY Rosi... her father moans as his sons guide him inside.

My Rosi, my Rosi... this macabre echo lingers as he vanishes.

Everyone looks, no one speaks. Father and brothers are like actors on a stage, the driveway is like the stands.

It's soundless outside as the brothers vanish. Vertiginously still for a few seconds that seem never to end.

Now the action moves inside. To the stage you can't see. And there's another stage, another scene taking place out of sight.

Nicolás.

Until just a moment ago, they were connected by a phrase like a silver thread: My Rosi, my Nicolás. Now that thread is broken. Nicolás has been expelled from the lamentation. Nicolás is no longer there, his name is no longer uttered. Rosi is the one who was killed. Rosi is the one who must be mourned.

My Rosi, my Rosi. *My Nicolás* will never be uttered again.

You stand alone in the driveway. Feeling the intermission has come. The first act is over as the brothers exit the stage, vanishing down the hallway with their father, and his voice reverberates, no longer uttering his son's name.

The scene takes place at dawn. The curtains fall, the lights come on.

For the first time, you start to tie up loose ends.

No longer, never again, is the question: Where are you, Nicolás?

Now, forever, over and over, it will be: Nicolás, what did you do?

The place is gone.

The cause remains. Why did you do it, Nicolás?

And then, again, the abyss, the darkness, the nothing engulfs you.

9

THE YEAR I spent in the woods of Tompkins County was a blank for my novel, for my fiction in general. I needed to disconnect from life in Murcia and go back to being the art historian I had ceased to be for the past few years. I reminded myself of the character in the novel I had just finished, Martín, an art historian who had abandoned the university for literature and who found a new opportunity at a research center in the United States. My writing had echoed into my existence; or what I had written had been a projection of the life I had wished to live.

At any rate, in Ithaca the character I was playing didn't open even once that notebook he had taken with him to make of himself a storyteller. And it had sounded so literary, telling people *I wrote my novel about the United States in Murcia, and I wrote my novel about the lowlands in the United States. I needed distance to write. To write about the near from afar and make a break with the place.* This wasn't possible. I didn't have the time or inclination. I needed to concentrate on reading and writing essays about art, temporality, and obsolescence and return to the art historian's task, the university professor's routine.

And I hoped to live my American adventure without looking back, particularly on that painful story.

And yet, the two times I returned to Murcia during the school year, the eclipsed past emerged once more to meet me, reminding me that it was still there, that it had no intention of leaving, and that I wouldn't escape it once I went back for good.

That November, I spent a few days in Spain for the Herralde Prize Ceremony. My novel, *The Instant of Danger*, was a finalist, and it was worth crossing the ocean to see this dream come true. Amid the tumult, I barely had time to speak to anyone. The interviews came in rapid succession, to the point that I ran out of things to say about the plot and what it meant to be runner-up for such an honor. When I arrived at the studio to speak with José Rocamora for Spanish Radio in Murcia just before my return to Ithaca, I had barely slept. The program lasted half an hour, and it was all I could do to keep myself upright. I drained the small bottle of water they'd given me, and halfway through, someone had to come in with another big one for me, a liter and a half. We talked about North American universities, my experience in Cornell, my difficulties with English, and balancing writing and teaching. When it was over, and I was on the verge of losing my voice, Rocamora, who had been my colleague when I was teaching at a private college, asked the inevitable question about what I was planning to write next.

"I've got something in mind," I answered hoarsely, "but it's still in the embryonic stage."

"Something about life in America, I assume."

"Something much closer to home," I countered. "A Murcian subject. I can't say anymore. It might bring bad luck, you know."

We finished, and Rocamora thanked me and asked if I could say a bit more now that the microphone was off. It intrigued him that I'd gone so far when what I wanted to examine was so close to home.

"Don't leave me hanging," he said. "I won't tell anyone. What's it about?"

I surprised myself by responding, "A murder in Murcia that happened twenty years ago. But I'm still in the documentation phase. In fact, I called here a while back looking for some footage from the regional news, but the people I spoke to all more or less blew me off."

"It's because the archives moved," he replied. Then, after a few seconds, he added, "But give me a minute and I'll put you in touch with someone on the TV side."

We walked into the vestibule, and he made a call from the information desk. Five minutes later, the news editor came down.

"Cati Martínez," she said, introducing herself.

I had read that name in the credits of Tele Murcia, but, I don't know why, I'd always imagined her much older.

Rocamora told her I was looking for a news broadcast from twenty years before for a book I was writing.

"Twenty years ago?" she asked.

"Yeah," I said, "from December of 1995."

"I don't know if it will still be around. They took almost all that stuff to Madrid, and what we have left is a total jumble. What do you need it for exactly?"

"I'm researching a murder. My friend killed his sister and then himself. And I gave a statement to a reporter and I'm looking for that tape. I want to see my past self face-to-face."

Her distant expression transformed when she heard these words. I don't know if it was the literary nature of what I was telling her. But Cati was ready to help and took down the date of the broadcast (December 26 or 27) and my cell number.

"It won't be easy, but I'll try. If it's there, I'll find it. Don't get your hopes up, though."

I thanked her and walked out, content, among other things, because I had the feeling I'd pushed the novel forward. It didn't matter so much whether or not she found the tape. What mattered was that I had tried, and if I ever told the story of my research, I could say that I'd dared to ask. It wasn't much at all, but it was something.

The morning before I returned to Ithaca, as I was packing my bag and printing my tickets, I got a call from Cati.

"We've got it," she said in her perfectly modulated voice. "It's about ten minutes long. Everyone's statements are there, including yours. *Miguel Ángel, friend of the accused.*"

I couldn't hide my excitement.

"You can come by and get it whenever you want."

"I'll be back in December," I said, "for Christmas. I need time to watch it and really digest it."

"Of course. I'll hold on to it for you. Safe travels."

After hanging up, I stood there thinking for a moment. I could have gone to the station that afternoon or even the next morning before flying out. But as I'd said, I needed time to digest it.

A month and a half later, I returned to Murcia for a few weeks for the holidays, and to promote my novel, which was now available in bookstores. Again, it was a whirlwind of interviews, events, lunches, dinners, reunions, drunken outings, and infinite hangovers. An endless party.

Throughout the celebrations, I was aware that the tape of the news broadcast was still waiting for me. On the flight to Murcia, I had told myself I'd call RTVE as soon as I landed. I had given Cati my word. But I kept putting it off, day after day, until I had to leave again and there was no more time to watch it.

It strikes me now that, in my heart, I didn't want to. Those images would have put a damper on the celebrations. It would have been like staring into the picture of Dorian Gray and running straight into the past. Maybe that's why I preferred to ignore it, go on carousing, savoring my success, being happy, enjoying myself, holding on to that moment of contentment before it vanished forever.

I didn't want to think of that time, and yet I felt guilty for looking away, especially during Christmas Eve dinner. Sitting at the table, it struck me that it was on that very same night, twenty years before, that everything had happened. And never in those twenty years, had I recalled that tragedy on that day. I had let Christmas remain Christmas, at least until Christmas, for other reasons, became a time of sorrow.

On Christmas Eve of 2002, Nena, who was practically a grandmother for me and my brothers, died in the middle of dinner. She was over ninety years old. The next year, at Christmas, despite his grief, my father put out the nativity scene and celebrated the holiday with the whole family, singing, drinking, and playing the tambourine. It was his favorite. Every year, before and after dinner, the children and grandchildren all gathered in front of the manger to sing Christmas carols. That year, instead of singing, my mother cried in her bedroom thinking about her aunt's death. Her aunt had been like a mother to her. She couldn't imagine that this would be the last time my father would sing with us. He would die the summer after, and Christmas would never be the same; we never put out the nativity scene, and we never had dinner together again. When my mother died four years later, Christmas Eve became a time for mourning and nostalgia.

Since then, I'd eaten with my wife's family, where I could laugh and pretend everything was fine and could toast to the future and to joys to come; but I never forgot the days when we used to gather in the big house and the whole farm was a celebration.

The Christmas Eve that I came home from Ithaca was the first one on which, instead of recalling lost joy and the family abode, I thought of the dark night when my friend killed his sister. When I flopped down exhausted in bed after gorging on nougat and cava, I looked at the clock and saw it was three-thirty in the morning. And I remembered how, twenty years before, my friend had done something terrible, unimaginable, at that very hour. At three-thirty, he had already murdered her. He was in his car driving away.

I struggled backward in my mind and tried to evoke everything about that night: what time I woke, what it was that made me get up out of bed, how I found out, what words were spoken. I forced myself to dredge it all back up. My room as a teenager. The darkness. I felt the curtains I sometimes had to reach out and touch to fall asleep. How did I wake? What was the first thing I heard? How did the nightmare begin?

It was then that I heard my father's voice. Deep. Gravelly. He was speaking to my mother. I paid attention and managed to make out his words: "Someone broke into Rosario's house, killed Rosi, and kidnapped Nicolás."

That was the start of everything. That was how this book needed to begin.

II

THE SEA OF FOG

DAWN BREAKS. IT'S cold. There's no point in spending any more time in the driveway. There's nothing to see there now.

Julia shows back up on the scene.

"Let's go to Asunción's house," she says, "her grandchildren are spending the night there."

She used this argument to convince you. Juan Carlos is there, and María José too. Julia knows you won't say no.

Your friends from Murcia. From the city. María José was born one day before you. Juan Carlos two years later. They came down on Saturdays and Sundays, and holidays too. They had the best toys. A Simon Speaks. A Festacolor movie projector. They had action figures. Leather balls. A basketball hoop hanging over the door to their backyard. Anything a boy could ever want. And when they came over, they always shared with you.

They come less often now. But today, they're here. They spent Christmas Eve at their grandparents' house, and they don't understand what's happened either.

Breakfast is on the table in the living room. They offer you a glass of chocolate milk and cookies. You're hungry, but you don't want María José to see you eating. You sit next to her on the sofa, and for a moment, everything stops.

She's always looked older. She's a grown woman now, people said. A woman who will never look at you in that way. You were the fat kid from the lowlands. She was the perfect city girl. But it didn't matter. You got over it soon enough. Still, you wanted to sit next to her. You always had. If you got a question in Trivial Pursuit or backheeled the soccer ball into the goalie's box, it wasn't to beat Juan Carlos or Nicolás, it was to get her to notice you for a few seconds, so you could look her in the eyes.

You never talked to Nicolás about that. There was never any rivalry there. You had the sense he wasn't interested in her. You never saw him look at her. Not the way you did. Never with desire, never with love. Or so you think, at least. Because now, you know you never could read Nicolás. Him or anybody else. But especially him.

1

I FOUND MYSELF back from Ithaca at the end of May 2016. My American adventure was over in the blink of an eye, and on my return, I had the sense that I had reached the end of something. My old routine was there waiting for me. I did not, like the hero of *The Instant of Danger*, return with a novel under my arm. But I did have a post at the university. A few days after returning, I passed the exam for a full professorship in Art History and had the sense that a new stage in my life was opening.

I needed to finish the essay on art that I had sketched out at Cornell. It was something I could have wrapped up in a couple of months. But once I was home, the story of my friend, the murder, took up all my thoughts and interrupted my other projects. I opened the black notebook I hadn't touched that entire year and reread the ideas, fragments, and drafts of the book I wished to write, and I saw very clearly that all of it was authentic and that it was this and not something else that I needed to work on. And so, one afternoon at the end of June, I shut myself up in my office, opened a file in Scrivener, and decided I would dedicate myself, body and soul, to the novel until it was done.

I wasn't sure where to start, but instinctively, I looked for the photos of Nicolás I had in the photo albums I'd brought from my parents' home and set them out on the desk. In a few of them, the two of us were together. School photos, field trips, first communion, Sunday school. That was all I had of him.

In most of the pictures, especially the ones from school, I could barely make out his face. Only in the Polaroids from communion were the two of us in the foreground. I was opening my mouth to receive the host, and he was looking at me askance.

His expression was serious, concentrated, his hair dark and glimmering, his long bangs overhanging his eyebrows. For a few minutes, I was hypnotized. Over time, I'd forgotten his face. In my memory, everything was imprecise. Nicolás was there, but he was blurry, and that day, looking at those photos, I tried to focus on his image and situate him onstage, in the place he had occupied for almost half my life.

As I began calling up the past, I decided to write down everything that came into my head. From that first day when I saw him in line for school to the afternoon before the Christmas Eve when the horror occurred, and he was sitting in the driveway playing chess with his cousin Pedro Luis. The two of us were always together. Sometimes there was a third. But he was always with me.

Nicolás and me up in a tree looking at each other in silence. Nicolás and me hiding in the river, waiting for intruders to come from the fields. Nicolás and me in the sacristy of the chapel preparing our readings. Nicolás and me on a field trip. Nicolás and me riding a bike to El Cabezo. Nicolás and me playing cards at his home. Nicolás and me in Sunday School. Nicolás and me...

The memories returned in flashes, I closed my eyes and traveled back to my youth. And yet I never stopped being there with my consciousness. I imagined what I could see or perceive in the past, but that act of imagination remained anchored in the present. I was there, but my vision wasn't mine, not exactly. It was the vision of the child I had been, of the man I have grown up to be. I saw this way, I thought of my memories in this way, in double time. The film with the director's commentary.

And in every memory was the stain of that night when the tragedy had happened, the darkness of it like a knife cutting into the flows of memory. A dense wall of fog with images projected on it like Chinese shadows, mingling with what had happened, taking on the somber texture of pain, the perplexity of the instant when Nicolás ceased to be my friend and became a monster.

INSIDE, EVERYTHING REVOLVES around Nicolás. Settled down on the sofa, you feel them sharing your pain. Juan Carlos and María José.

They never threatened what the two of you had because they always showed up and left. They shared their toys, and you lent them the lowlands.

The lowlands, your place, your playing field, your secret paradise. Until the village kids showed up and discovered your sandpile, your tree, and your gate, your goalie's box without a crossbar.

The village kids. You remember them perfectly.

You were ten years old. A day comes when they show up and park their bikes. Seven of them. They're older. They take away your ball. They insult you. They threaten you and say they'll be back the next day.

For the first time, you feel vulnerable. Under watch. Your paradise threatened. Your perfect peace and quiet on the verge of being torn apart.

The next day, you don't dare leave home, but you plan how to defend your territory. You spend the day thinking of strategies. You're the one who comes up with the plan. Nicolás says nothing, but he obeys your orders.

You cut out paper arrows and write on them, *Come and get us if you've got the balls.* You spread them out on the road, creating a trail to the site of the ambush.

You hide in the cane brakes by the river. The perfect lookout. That afternoon, you're not scared of the snakes and the rats. In the cane, you feel safe. The cane is your territory.

You wait there until naptime, with cane cut in the shape of arrows and bags full of jagged rocks. When they show up on the narrow road, you'll attack. They'll learn their lesson. They won't bother you again.

For hours, you wait in silence. Hidden. Anticipating the moment of battle. You're nervous. You look at each other and smile, thinking of your perfect plan. Everything's justified. This will be your grandiose revenge.

Hours pass, and night starts to fall. You're hungry, but you remain there in silence. Expectation transforms to fear. Might they have sensed the ruse? Will they come from elsewhere, catching you off guard?

When you no longer believe anyone will come, you hear voices from far off and ready yourselves for the attack.

The voices are jumbled together, and it takes you time to tell them apart.

Then you put down your stones and spears and step out of the cane brake.

"Are y'all stupid?" your brother Juan asks.

Your mother jerks your forearm and smacks you several times on the behind. You don't open your mouth. Nicolás's mother takes him by the hand. She doesn't hit him. She doesn't say anything to him either.

"Who were you hiding from?" your mother asks.

You look at each other. You wait in silence. This is your war. And you're returning home defeated.

The village kids didn't come that day. They didn't come back the next day either, or in the weeks and months that followed. But the fear was always there. An invisible enemy that could strike at any time. Your hiding place had been discovered. And the bag of sharp stones remained always with you. A weapon for emergencies. For any threat that might arise.

You still remember where you hid them.

You feel tempted to go look for them.

2

I SPENT DAYS shut up in my office. I wrote out in one stretch all that came into my head, one scene after the other, in no chronological order, with no idea what to do with them. I assumed I would place these things somewhere in the novel. Or maybe I wouldn't even use them. I wasn't worried about it at the time.

As I thought back, I was surprised at my feeling of distance and detachment, as if Nicolás and the murder hardly mattered and those memories were just random episodes from my life. I was incapable of reinstating the emotions I had felt. I described them as if they were in a movie, not managing to penetrate them. They were fixed images that hardly touched me. Or that touched me only when they wanted to, and not when I decided.

I couldn't reconstruct what I'd once felt for Nicolás either. I wanted to, I wanted to say what about him had mattered to me, what it meant to learn of what he'd done, what it meant to lose him forever. I realized I would never do so faithfully, though, that the past might never reverberate in the present with the intensity that it once had. It was buried too deep now, hidden too far away for me to awaken it. And yet, cold, frozen, those years started to come back to me. To my days and, above all, to my nights.

It was then that the nightmares began. In them, I managed to feel the past quiver, the distance dissolve, the walls I had built to close off that time crumble into dust.

I've never paid much attention to dreams in literature. They've always seemed a facile way of pushing the narrative forward and imbuing it with a measure of mystery. And yet, those nightmares struck me with such force that I couldn't look away from them. I woke from them in a state of shock, sweaty and ill at ease, and that uneasiness wouldn't vanish the entire morning following. Sleep and wakefulness formed a continuity, and I lived whole days in memory, trying to dominate the past, while at night, that past dominated me in dreams.

I couldn't help jotting down one of them in a notebook:

We're in the yard. All my friends from childhood: Roberto, Silvestre, Pedro Luis, Nicolás, and me. We're playing a game, but I'm not sure what. Basketball, I think. He hugs me tight. And he says he only wants to be with me. He wants everyone else to leave. He tells me he loves me. I am moved, and I tell him I love him too. He comes close and kisses me. I turn away, and he looks surprised. We start playing again, but everything's changed. Everyone's scared of him. There's something invisible there that everybody can sense. I recognize then that I've brought him back to life, and I regret it, because I've created something malignant.

I feel a strange force. There's water everywhere. I wake up with a dry mouth.

Since Christmas of 1995, I've dreamed of Nicolás several times. He always appears as if nothing unusual had happened. I'm happy to see him. Sometimes I even wake up with tears in my eyes. In the nightmares I had since starting the novel, I was still pleased that he was alive, but I always found something strange, perverse in his behavior, and my pleasure quickly turned to regret. Being with him again was unnatural. I had resuscitated him. And the guilt ate me alive.

Those were upsetting dreams. But even worse were the nightmares about his sister Rosi. I had never dreamed of her before. But as soon as the book progressed, she became an increasingly frequent visitor at night.

One of the nightmares I recall with special torment. It was probably the most vivid one I've ever had. Maybe because it came to me in the midst of a methamphetamine hangover and my perceptions were altered in a way they never had been. It happened after a writer friend's wedding. I saw shadows for nights on end, and every time I closed my eyes, all that was in my mind seemed real. My nightmares were part of that reality.

In this dream, I am visiting a grave at a cemetery. But the grave is at El Cabezo de la Plata. At the same time, it's on the farm, or in a liminal space, a dry field and a verdant garden at the same time. The coffins laid out there for all to see. I walk into a room to leave flowers for them. When I reach her casket, I see a crack in it and I can glimpse her legs, which are covered in cuts and bruises. The wounds start to bleed. She rises up and stares at me. She asks, "Do you not see my wounds?" I try to leave, but my body won't move. I ask her forgiveness and manage to get away. Outside—now I am clearly back on the farm—I start to cry.

My mother's there, and she comes over to console me. "Did you see Rosi?" she asks. "Did you notice whether she was pregnant?" I don't know what to say, and I run away from her too. I'm trying to leave, but I keep returning to the same place, something has changed, though: Rosi is no longer in her coffin, she's in a chair, observing a kind of funeral, and all of us must say something about the dead. When it's my turn, I say that I love Nicolás, that I always have, that he's my best friend. As I talk, I can feel Rosi's eyes on me. Her body is covered in dust. I ask her how long she's been there. "Since the first night," she says. "I clean the tomb and I change the water in the flowers. I always have."

My mother enters the vault just then. She kisses Rosi's face and touches her chin. "Ay, Rosi . . . ," she says.

Then, unexpectedly, Rosi produces a knife, rises from her chair, and walks toward me. Her legs are still bleeding. Her wounds look like the lashes of a whip. Her skin is open. Again, I try to escape. She raises the knife, less in an attacking posture than defensively, and shouts, louder and louder, "Go to my house! Go to my house! Go to my house!" I am five years old. I am on my blue bicycle with the training wheels. In the garden, next to her house. Nicolás is nowhere to be seen. And her words keep echoing in my head. Her scream is now a murmur, now a screech, now an earthquake making everything shake.

I am awakened by the machine cleaning the streets. My eyes are damp. I write the dream down before I forget it, without knowing yet what it signifies.

THEY FOUND THE car at El Cabezo de la Plata. Next to a house Rosario owns.

Juan Carlos and María José's grandfather says this. And everyone starts speculating.

Why would they take him there, to El Cabezo? Maybe the family had money squirreled away up there. Maybe they forced him to go. They showed up to rob the place and they couldn't find anything worth stealing. Rosi burst in and they killed her. And they took Nicolás up to El Cabezo because they thought maybe there was money there.

Nothing makes any sense. But you don't stop speculating. And the most obvious thing passes through no one's head. Because the most obvious thing makes even less sense.

El Cabezo. You know where it is. The village on top of the mountain. You've been up there more than once to play with Nicolás and his cousin Juan Alberto.

You go there on your bikes, but you can never pedal up the last few hills. You always get off and finish the climb on foot. It's an adventure. Four miles uphill. Nicolás always in front, setting the pace. You behind, trying to follow. He never looks back. He doesn't care. He never brakes, never turns around. Not even that day when you fall and break a finger on your left hand. Nicolás keeps pedaling, continues on his way until he reaches his destination. Only then does he get off and look at you with disbelief.

In El Cabezo, you walk along the waterways and your shoes get caked in mud. El Cabezo is another paradise. Like the lowlands. Another secret. A secret Nicolás knows perfectly. Like his parents' place up there. That's the one thing you've never seen, that property. You know it exists, but he's never told you where it is.

And so now you can't imagine where they found the car. All you can think of is a field. An abstract field. On a road next to an almond grove.

Someone took him there in the car. That's what you try to tell yourself. But you can't, not anymore. Try as you might. Wish as you might. You can no longer imagine Nicolás in the back seat, gagged, pointing the way. Or up front, with a pistol pointed at his head, driving to his parents' property. No. In your mind, Nicolás drives alone. In your mind, he parks the car, opens the door, and starts to run. No one took him there. Nicolás escaped. You sense why, but you still don't want to consider it.

3

"**THE CALENDAR PAGES** were turning on their own," my sister-in-law Mari Carmen said. "Julia never said anything about it? She knows how scary it was."

"She never mentioned it," I responded.

My brother Emilio had organized a family meal at home, and when lunch was over, after hearing the story of my trip to Ithaca, my sister-in-law had told me to listen close to her if I really wanted to describe what had happened in the lowlands. There were things I needed to know. Among them, that not long after the night of the murder, strange things began happening. Calendars rustled, lights flickered on, noises emerged from empty houses.

"There was a lingering negative energy," she concluded. "I was tempted to call a team of paranormal investigators to channel them or do a karmic cleansing or something like that."

She was being serious, and it was no surprise, because she and my brother were great believers in the paranormal, and from the moment they learned I'd be writing a novel about what had happened there, they assumed I'd be writing about spirits, phantoms, spectral voices, and diabolical energies. Funny enough, my brother had started drafting a short novel about the events a while earlier. He had never written anything before, but the story obsessed him, so much so that he dug out from storage an old portable Olivetti that had shown up from who knew where and would type a few pages late at night, just before going to bed. He told me later that when he was writing, he noticed a mist forming around him, and fear gripped him, and he burned his manuscript and tried to put everything out of his mind. He let me read a passage or two before then, to tell him what I thought. I only remember the beginning: *The devil has come to the lowlands. He's watching us through the windows. He waits for us in every corner. We can no longer escape him.*

I was a believer for a time as well. We used to watch horror movies, chant formulas to make the dead from urban legends appear in mirrors; we were convinced we were surrounded by phantoms and forces from the beyond, we believed in horoscopes and tarot cards and used to look into the sky for signs of extraterrestrial civilizations. That mysterious world, which strikes me now as so outlandish, was always with us. It was real. It existed. We felt it. I remember the fear and unease that night when my sister-in-law called to alert us to something strange that had landed in the garden. A light crossed the sky and fell over the stand of lemon trees in front of the house. The TV turned staticky, and the dog, a normally even-tempered Belgian Shepherd, wouldn't stop barking. My brother Juan grabbed the shotgun, filled it with shells, and walked outside. Behind him, Emilio was shining a flashlight, and I trailed them with an iron bar. I don't know how old I was, fourteen or fifteen, but I do remember my brother's words perfectly:

"Juan, for God's sake, if you see something, don't shoot. You could spark off an interplanetary war."

There was nothing there. No tracks, no char marks, nothing burnt. The dog kept barking, though. And the next day, he died.

It was like a movie, that scene of us walking out into the yard in the middle of the night. Our minds were filled with images from *Predator*, *The Thing*, all those movies where a strange object falls from the sky in the middle of nowhere and destroys everything in its path. It didn't matter if what was happening there was real or not, if there was or wasn't anything there. We were stepping into the unknown, and we couldn't help being terrified.

In later years, I stopped believing. But I remain fascinated by films about ghosts and extraterrestrials and the idea that there is a world beyond ours, beyond the tangible, material, confirmable universe. Nor do I look down on the idea. I'm not closed off to it. I leave open the possibility. There must be something, after all. But I prefer not to think about it.

But what I wanted to write was neither a horror novel nor a ghost story. Or at least the ghosts, the voices from the past, the disturbing images, wouldn't belong to the paranormal world. I had, however, spent the recent weeks surrounded by apparitions: spirits, phantoms, voices, the dead coming back to life. In dreams and in memory.

I didn't tell my sister-in-law this. I didn't tell her Rosi bled in my nightmares or that Nicolás was hiding something awful inside him and seemed possessed by a demonic force. She'd have taken all of that as signs from the beyond. And maybe she was right. But in a different way. It was my own sense of guilt that was speaking through them. The dead returned because I opened their coffins, because my writing and memories resuscitated them. My novel was the Ouija board that summoned them. I had brought them back. Maybe the things on my desk didn't move on their own, maybe the doors didn't slam shut unexpectedly. But Rosi and Nicolás were watching. I felt them behind me as I wrote. They dwelled in my mind when I slept. They were with me at all hours.

After dinner, my wife went home and I spent a few more hours on the farm. My brother Emilio said he'd drive me back later. It was hot, but I wanted to walk the paths I'd known in childhood. Writing all those memories down had revived the need to see again those places I had evoked. The past had returned to my mind in force, and I wanted to synchronize it with the present.

I walked down the road in front of what had once been Julia's house, and in ten minutes, I'd reached the river. Everything had changed. The river wasn't even there anymore. After the constant flooding, the regional government had decided to change the course of the river, and in the early nineties, they filled in many of its offshoots. That was before the murder, but in my mind, the river had still been running then, at least I saw it there whenever I thought of Nicolás. Now it was just a flat expanse of land. I imagined the games we could have played there if it had been like that when we were young.

On one of the near-lying properties, a neighbor had opened an RV park. The road, which had always been empty, was now filled with tourists from Spain and other countries on the weekends. I ran into some on the way, and I wondered what we'd have felt as children hearing people there speaking French, English, or German. I thought of all that had disappeared, but I also projected the present I saw around me into our past. How would our childhood in the lowlands have been if these changes had happened back then?

Memory is a question of scale. And now everything was different in size. I remembered the tree we used to climb to while away our dead hours, talking or waiting in silence for the sun to go down. It wasn't so tall; I'd been little in those days, and I never had the brawn to climb very high. Now, I thought, it must look minuscule.

Where was it exactly? I thought for a moment. An orchard at the end of the road, close to the river, on a corner, in what would have passed for the heart of the forest.

As I walked, I kept telling myself that I wanted to see the tree, climb it again, check how much my sense of scale had changed. But that would never happen. The tree wasn't there, nor the orchard, nor were the borders the same, nor was the road. A concrete slab had erased it all. A chalet surrounded by an iron fence sealed off all sight of where they once had lain.

I walked to the gate and heard children splashing in the pool. What part of that house had been built over that tree from our childhood? Poetically, I liked to think it was the pool where the children were playing that stood atop the memory of our former watchtower. But I couldn't tell. It was impossible to impose my mental map on that new space. I did think the one place had been superimposed on the other, and that somewhere, those two worlds must touch.

I thought of what Pierre Nora called *lieux de mémoire*, sites of memory. Since the nineties, especially, the humanities had taken an interest in those areas that contained what the French historian called *dominant memory*. Battlefields, ruins, places of mnemonic density... But what about the other places, those where the remembered was insignificant? It occurred to me then that any inhabited place could be a *lieu de mémoire*. That vanished tree was one. At least for me. For Nicolás too, I supposed. There, the two of us stood above the world. Would anything of that energy be left in the chalet now standing there? I doubt the owners of the place will ever look through this book. But if, for some strange reason, it should fall into their hands and they should read this paragraph, they will know that on the parcel of land their home now occupies, two children climbed a tree and believed themselves fortunate and happy.

I walked back to the trailhead and saw Julia's old house. That was another *lieu de mémoire.* And there, too, little of the past remained. The new buyers hadn't touched the façade, but they had completely renovated the interior. I remember how it hurt Julia when she had to move away.

The house shared and still shares a wall with the one where Nicolás lived. I went there almost every day, walking through the orchards in the back. For the last stretch, I took a narrow path that ran past the house and was only visible from two windows: Rosi's and Nicolás's. I always hurried through there, trying to avoid the wasps that swarmed in hundreds of nests they'd built in the hollows of the bare bricks. It was a rare week when I didn't get stung, especially in the summer.

After failing to find that tree from my childhood, I turned toward that path that had been a constant presence in my youth. The bricks were all plastered over now, all the chinks filled. The wasps must be gone now too, I thought. Night hadn't yet fallen, but between the shadow of the house and the shadow of the trees, it was dark there. I could hear the cicadas' far off hum and the call of a bird I didn't know the name of. Again it all seemed so much smaller than I remembered. The branches of the lemon trees nearly touched the walls of the house, and there was hardly room to walk. But I decided to push my way through, stopping a few seconds under the window of the room where it all happened. I thought of what Rosi had said in one of my dreams: *Come to my house, come to my house.* At that moment, I felt the hairs stand up on the nape of my neck and I felt uneasy. What was I doing there? What was I looking for? What did I want to see, hear, or feel?

I remembered what my sister-in-law had said. A malign force. Something unsettling. I don't know if that's what I perceived. But the sensation was disconcerting, and I walked faster. The ten or so seconds it took to cross that short path were eternal. The wasps had vanished, but I felt my body ravaged by stings, as if all those I'd ever received through the years on that stretch of land all began to throb again at once.

It was fear. I know that now. The sting of time.

SOMETHING STARTS TO move offscreen. You hear it from inside the house. A murmur, a mood you can perceive even from the living room.

Don't go out, someone says.

They try to close the door to the street, but you manage to peek out. And in the distance, you can see it. The body.

Her body, on a stretcher, covered by a gray cloth.

Go back inside, don't look, don't go out.

But you can't help it. The body draws all stares to it. Yours, and the stares of those in the driveway.

Again it is a movie. But there is no dramatic music. Just the silence of muted gestures. And the creak of the wheels of the stretcher. The dull thud as it goes down the back stairs. The thud that shakes the entire body, which is held down with bands.

They close the door, and the car departs. You remain on the threshold. For the first time, you think of Rosi. She was offscreen. And now, at last, she appears. Veiled. Hidden. At the limits of the visible.

You still don't know—you don't even sense it—but

that image will never leave your mind. The corpse of your friend's sister. Your most feared secret. Under every sheet over every veiled Christ and every covered body. The shape of all ghosts.

4

WHEN I RETURNED to my brother's house after my walk through the lowlands, the sun was going down, and Emilio was dragging some chairs out onto the patio. His posture, as he did so, reminded me of my father. His long legs, the way he swayed from side to side, his stern, focused expression. Of the four of us, he was the one who most resembled Dad.

"Feel like sitting down a while before I take you home?" he asked when he saw me. "Juan's on his way over. He just went to feed the chickens, he'll be right back."

"Where?"

"Our parents' place. Haven't you seen? He's turned the backyard into a henhouse."

"At least someone's using it for something," I said.

My brother stared at me briefly and replied, "Honestly, it breaks my heart when I think about it."

"Sure," I answered, excusing myself. "I'm going to take a look and see what he's done."

I walked a few yards to the house at the end of the road, the one I'd lived in until I left at twenty-six years of age. That was the whole of my inheritance. The house goes to the youngest one. After my mother's death, it was empty, and it started to fall apart. I deceived myself for a while, telling myself I'd fix it up and start going back there on the weekends, but soon I had to admit I'd never even do that. The only solution was to try to rent it. But even then, it needed repairs and renovations I couldn't afford. And so, to keep it from sinking into the ground, I lent it to some neighbors who needed a place to stay for a little more than a year, with the condition that they take care of it and pay the bills. It didn't work out as planned, and afterward, I turned off the water, the electricity, and the phone and chalked it up as a loss.

Still, that evening, when I went to see what my brother had done, and when I saw the chicken coop he'd built between the patio and the shed, I couldn't help but feel something squirming within me. That was where my mother used to cook, where in wintertime she would go out to make breakfast for my father and my brothers when they had to go to work early.

"You don't mind, do you?"

"Of course not," I responded. "If it's all going to just sit here and rot, it's better for someone to make use of it."

I really did think that. And yet I couldn't rid myself of a certain remorse. It was my fault and my fault alone that the house was rotting. I was the one who had let it go to waste. But the world isn't a museum, sometimes things collapse under their own weight, and all you can do is stand there and watch them crumble. That's what I told myself—what I'm still telling myself—as consolation for failing to pay attention to the relics of my childhood and of several generations.

As my brother finished feeding the chickens, I was drawn inside the house, where I walked around for a few minutes. I hadn't been in there for years, maybe not since its last inhabitants moved to the village. It was strange to see the living room exactly as it had been the day my mother died. The chairs, the couch, the table, the television, the crockery in the cabinets, the figures on top of the refrigerator... Either the acquaintances I had lent the place to had adapted to what was already there, barely moving anything in their time there, or else these things had returned of their own accord, with a life of their own, retaking their home, the places that had belonged to them forever.

The rocking chairs still stood around the table with the brasier in its base, just where they'd always been, looking toward the window that opened onto the trail. Seeing them like that gave me a direct view into the past. A stage setting without people. The body of things.

One of those chairs had belonged to Nena until she died. Then to my father, until the thrombosis killed him. The other, the one closer to the window, was my mother's. Thrombosis got her too, in the end, but really, it was depression. Years and years of it. That is the ineffaceable image of the living room. Sundown outside, the curtain drawn, the light dim, the shadows thick. And my mother sitting there, rocking in slow motion, gaze lost, hands limp in her lap. The black sun of illness creeping through the house.

I couldn't say when it all began. In my memory, my mother's depression was constant, but worse in autumn and spring. In those months, that lovely, tall, resolute woman became a withered body that could hardly utter a word. The memories of those days are like sepia film stills constantly repeated. Hair dirty in her face, sorrowful expression, empty eyes, dark circles beneath them, prolonged silences. And in the morning, the Xanax and Ativan next to the glass of milk and the cookies, floating on the transparent plastic tablecloth that covered the crochet one beneath it. And her peculiar way of slipping the pills into her mouth. Index and middle fingers like pincers, reaching toward the back of her throat. Eyes closed during the sip of milk.

And my father's anguished interrogation.

"What the hell's wrong with you, Emilia?"

"Nothing, Juan Antonio, nothing."

"Then get a damn grip! Your children and grandchildren are healthy, your family loves you, your husband's got a decent job. . . . You've got a house, a TV, your whole life's worked out. Are you not happy? Do you have some reason not to be?"

"I don't know, Juan Antonio. I don't know what's wrong with me."

And she must not have. No one else did either. Maybe there was no reason. Or at least no reason that could be mentioned.

I remember the frustration. The desperation. Not understanding. Not knowing what to do. And the thought that kept hovering over our heads: She's selfish. Mom is selfish. That's what we thought, and what we let drop occasionally in conversations: Depression was a way of getting attention, she neglected herself and used her sorrow to play the victim, how childish, when she cries, she gets to be the center of the world.

And maybe there was some of that. But not in the way we believed. I've thought about this a lot in the intervening years, and more and more, I'm sure that my mother's depression was an unconscious way of getting our attention because she needed to be cared for, because she was crying out no longer to be everyone's slave. She had devoted her entire life to serving others. She took care of her older aunts and uncles, and later, of her kids. And then of her husband. She never left the house in the lowlands, not even when my father had to go to Alicante for work for several years. I always thought she should have gone with him, that they should have built a home there. A young couple with two newborn children and their entire life ahead of them. But my mother stayed in Murcia, took care of her children, took care of her unmarried uncles, took care of the house, took care of her heritage, prisoner to a way of life with roots that sank deep into the past.

All that must have taken its toll on her, that life devoted to others, those years of confinement, all the frustration, all the lost happiness, all the gathered melancholy, and these things came back later in the form of depression.

"She's sad," a healer said when we had despaired of the doctors and decided to try something else.

Now, when I think about it, I believe she was right. Deep down, that was all there was to it. She was sad.

And with that sadness that never left her, my mother took care of Nena in her last years, dressing her, feeding her, changing her diapers, keeping an eye on her, never going outside so Nena wouldn't be alone, repeating these routines until the day she died. Then, not six months later, my father's thrombosis left him practically bedbound. We used to sit him in the rocking chair Nena had sat in, and my mother would take care of him. She dressed him, fed him, changed his diapers, never left him alone. It was as if the past were repeating itself. Later, the wheel spun again, and this time, it was her turn.

I still have the video I recorded the evening before her stroke. I was in the room I had built onto one corner of the house to have some solitude, and she came in to tell me dinner was ready. Her face was gaunt, her eyes sunken, her voice hardly audible.

I remember our conversation perfectly.

"Mom, you look terrible."

"I'm sad, son. I can't do it anymore."

The next morning, as I was writing in my office at the university, I got the call. My mother was in the hospital, the left side of her body paralyzed, and she couldn't talk.

She would never be the same person again. She couldn't even cry a few months later when my father died.

This is all a long time ago now. Increasingly, I'm convinced we were to blame. My brothers and I. For what happened to our mother. We had perpetuated the long tradition of her servitude. We used her until she couldn't take it anymore. We left her alone with an inherited burden, and eventually, it did her in.

Strangely, the last years of her life, when she could no longer care for herself, were the only ones when she never had to serve anybody. The only ones when someone else took care of her. But not us. Her sons didn't pay back her selflessness. Not in the same way, anyhow. We didn't give up our lives for her or sacrifice our happiness as she had done. Times had changed and children no longer looked after their parents. It would have been different, I suppose, if one of us had been a woman. Then the submission would have continued. After all, this was still the lowlands. Daughters did take care of their elders. We were all sons, though, and we couldn't change our routines to look after our mother. So we left it all in the hands of *the girls.* The girls were two Ecuadorians, three Bolivians, and last of all, a Bulgarian. One after the other. Until they decided they couldn't keep doing it. Twenty-four hours a day, morning and night, with weekends off. That was all the commitment we could manage: sporadic visits, and then each of us stayed with her one weekend a month. One for each brother. The minimal heroism of bathing her, changing her diapers, giving her medicine, giving her food, keeping her company, taking her out for a walk. One weekend. Until the end.

That evening, when I went to see what Juan had done, I felt, once more, the gray heft of illness. Sorrow, anguish, and desperation still suffused every corner of the house and every corner of my memories. It was hard for me to recall laughter or moments of happiness there, as if some viscous mass stood between me and whatever brightness might lie beyond it. Only now, as I write these paragraphs, do I begin to sense other energies nestled in the history of that place. Moments buried by disconsolateness, luminous memories drowned out by the murmur of affliction.

I force myself to dredge them up now, to think of myself there, with my mother, Nena, and my father, sitting around the table with the brazier, feeling the warmth from the freshly lit coals, watching *Knight Rider*, *The Greatest American Hero*, or *Street Hawk* after the news, clutching the coins Nena used to slip me, which no one ever knew about, laughing at the jokes my father would tell in his Andalusian accent, or staying up late to watch *My Favorite Terrors* by Chicho Ibáñez Serrador, ignoring the *For Mature Audiences Only* and not really understanding what was going on. The four of us there in the living room, in the present, knowing nothing of the future, unaware that what we were brushing against in those moments was something like bliss.

YOU LINGER ON the threshold. You don't cross it until the hearse drives away. The body leaves the scene, and you walk out to the driveway.

Your father and brother are still there by the gate. You approach them, and your father hugs you.

There's no justice in the world, he says. That poor boy, that poor girl. Murderers. Murderers.

Your brother grabs him by the arm: Dad, don't you get it? Nobody burst in there and killed Rosi.

What do you mean?

There was no break-in. The killer was inside. Surely to God you can see that?

Your father doesn't respond. Nor do you say anything. No one wants to, in their hearts, because to say it is to make it reality. And if no one dares say it, it hasn't fully happened.

At a certain point, someone speaks. You don't know who it is at first. But someone utters the phrase: It was him, the brother. He's the one who killed her.

And afterward, there are no more whispers. The voices of the lowlands can be heard.

Son of a bitch. Psycho. Son of a bitch.

He beat her to death. He took off in the car. He escaped. The Civil Guard's looking for him.

Son of a bitch. Murderer. Bastard. Psycho. Killing his sister. Murderer. Bastard. Psycho.

The lowlands are in a frenzy. They know now who the enemy is. All that time, they'd been waiting. But now they've found out who's guilty.

Murderer. Bastard. Psycho.

Only your father and your brother say nothing.

Go back where you were, Miguel.

Son of a bitch. Bastard.

You can feel their eyes on you.

That's his friend. The killer's friend.

You close your ears and return to Asunción's house. There, too, they've heard everything. They know everything. But there, Nicolás is still a friend.

You sit on the sofa. You look at Juan Carlos. You look at María José. You look at Julia.

Don't believe them, she starts to say.

But she can't finish the phrase.

5

AT THE END of July, I finally decided to look at the papers in the municipal archives. I had spent weeks writing down memories and sketching out drafts and ideas for the structure of the novel, and I couldn't delay searching for proper information any longer.

It wasn't the first time I'd been there. In the last year of my degree, I went there often to do research. I still didn't know which direction my work would take, and following the advice of a professor, I looked into something I found interesting, even if it wasn't my passion: the fate of religious sculptures in Murcia after the destruction of the Spanish Civil War. For more than a year, I combed through all the regional newspapers looking for stories about sculptures being blessed during the reconstruction that followed *the red barbarism.* I had several blue folders I filled with notes and clippings.

I admit I never wanted to be an archival researcher. I soon gave up that kind of art history for another that was more comfortable, with new books instead of dusty papers—but I recognize that archives held a hypnotic fascination. As I dug around looking for accounts of sculptures recently purchased, which would reveal something about the ones that had been destroyed, I felt like William of Baskerville in *The Name of the Rose*. A detective investigating a crime. In my case, the crime was devastation, and I would learn what the flames had consumed by examining what was put in their place. After all my work, all I published was a small article on the iconography of the Sacred Heart as a metaphor in Francoist rhetoric. Fortunately that text can no longer be found.

The July morning when I went to the archives, I remembered the past with nostalgia. Back then I had investigated a symbolic crime—the destruction of icons—and now I was back looking into a real one, as a detective rather than as a historian. I was no longer in search of days past or snooping at random. I wasn't an intruder from the present tracing out a past I had no connection to. I was trying to find a fragment of my own history. I had been there. I was looking into a part of my past.

I asked for newspapers from 1995. The archivist told me some had been digitized. By law, because the contents were copyrighted, they couldn't be examined online, but I could examine them on the computers in the research room.

It was easy. I had the dates, and I knew where the story had been published: in *La Verdad*, *La Opinión*, and *Diario 16*, which were the three local papers in Murcia at the time.

I examined that week's stories in detail. On Tuesday, December 26, 1995, all of them bore the disaster on their front page: *Christmas Eve Tragedy in the Lowlands. A Young Man from Los Ramos Kills Sister and Leaps off Cliff. Christmas of Death in Murcia. The Cain of Murcia.* The next day there were briefer mentions, and then the case was forgotten forever. I flipped through the pages that discussed the crime, but didn't waste time with the articles. I'd have time to read them carefully later. What I did was page through them—or scroll, in the case of *La Verdad*—to try and remember what the world was like in 1995.

The news of the day was a speech given on Christmas Eve, with King Juan Carlos calling for all sides to unite in the fight against ETA terrorism. The next day, the Basque police took down the Alava Commando shortly before they attacked. That same day, Juan Guerra was sentenced to two years in jail for tax fraud in the amount of forty-two million pesetas. And, at the end of the week, President Felipe González confirmed that the next elections would be held in March of the following year. "I am worried about the difficulties Spain will face if it falls into Aznar's hands," he said at the press conference.

I no longer remembered any of that. Only the soccer scores for Madrid and Murcia felt familiar, and the movie premieres: *Babe* and *Goldeneye.* I didn't watch the news or read the papers back then. My world was just me and those around me. I wasn't interested in politics. I didn't know anything. I was just a kid from the lowlands who was going to college in the capital and didn't give a damn how things worked.

As I read that morning, I felt a strange melancholy. More than remembering the world of the past, I had the feeling I was coming to know it for the first time.

YOU'RE SITTING ON the couch, in silence, waiting for something. You don't know what.

No one says a word, but everyone's starting to realize. It's here and now that Nicolás starts to become a murderer. Even if no one dares to acknowledge it.

They're onto him, someone says through the window.

The expression haunts you. They're not looking for him anymore. They haven't lost him. Now they're onto him. Nicolás is running away. From the Civil Guard, from the local police, from the people in El Cabezo, maybe from some neighbor from the lowlands who's gotten in his car and joined the search party. Hunting down the killer.

You can't stop thinking about him scurrying across the fields, jumping over sudden drops, dodging the weeds, looking for a hiding place. Somewhere he can breathe.

Run, Nicolás. Hide. Don't let them catch you.

You surprise yourself with these thoughts. And you feel you're on his side. The side of the murderer. Because in your mind, he's still your friend.

Nicolás is the hunted. He's a frightened child. He's your friend, and he has no skin, no one and nothing that can protect him.

6

AT HOME, I printed the documents and read them carefully. All of them repeated the same information: "The sister's body was found by her mother in a puddle of blood." "The young woman's room showed clear signs of struggle." "After fleeing, the young man initially tried to hang himself." Details of the events, but also of the search: "Dozens of neighbors looked for the suspect in the area around Alquerías. The search focused on the mountains, on a rugged area, in the darkness of night, and as the hours passed, neighbors continued to join, until dozens of people were participating."

I imagined the scene, and it reminded me of movies where the whole town corners a monster and he flees in fear. I thought of Nicolás racing through the rocky hills, trying to hide from everyone, hearing shouts in the distance, sensing his pursuers. Trying, above all, to run from himself, from that inner monster he'd let out.

Nothing I read was new to me, apart from some of the information about the Civil Guard investigation and the judge who ordered the bodies to be transferred to the Institute for Forensic Medicine in Murcia for autopsy.

Many articles lingered on the scandalous details—how her body had been found, the pool of blood in the bedroom, the height of the cliff Nicolás had jumped from—but most homed in on something that would be repeated over and over: the inability of the neighbors to believe what had happened.

All the statements coincided on this point. The headline of an article in *La Verdad* put it thus: "A timid boy, liked by all . . . No one could believe that Nicolás, that eighteen-year-old everyone had gotten along with and treasured since he was a child and served as altar boy in the local church, had taken his life on that cliff and was the main suspect in the bludgeoning death of his sister Rosi, not long after the family's Christmas Eve dinner."

All emphasized the neighbors' surprise: "When the question arises as to why, everyone says the same thing: 'It's impossible to think about why. After what's happened, in all honesty, I still don't understand a thing.'"

The article in *La Verdad*, signed by the reporter Alfonso Torices, ends on a poetic note: "More than one person thinks the reason behind the quarrel may have died with the brother and sister."

Looking back at the news led me to experience again that strange incredulity, that pain, the intensity, the searching, the unsettledness . . . the images, especially, shook me, above all the high cliffside splashed across the cover of *La Verdad*. *The sixty-foot drop the young man jumped from*, the photo caption read. At the top of the cliff were two small figures. I could recognize one of them: Juan Alberto in his dark green tracksuit, observing the terrain where he had discovered his cousin's body.

For a moment, I was hypnotized as I looked at the photograph. Those two figures staring straight into the abyss reminded me of the paintings of Caspar David Friedrich.

The cliff, the immensity of nature, the leap, the suicide...the tragic death of a tormented being, it eclipsed everything else. The paper had opened with the place Nicolás had jumped from—not his sister's coffin, not the house, not the room where everything happened. And all this overwhelmed reason, spilling over into the irrational and the incomprehensible. Surely the editor didn't realize it, but he had imposed an interpretation on what had happened: tragedy, an unimaginable crime, something no one can grasp. Just like those figures peering over the cliff's edge into the distance. Everyone was paralyzed, no one understood. Walkers before a sea of fog.

I read all the articles closely, as if I were a historical researcher and had to interpret the text in an exercise in cultural hermeneutics. The idea of my friend's tragic death had eclipsed the murder. He was the main character of the story. His sister, the victim, was an extra.

It was strange that none of the newspapers made even a single allusion to terms like domestic violence, gender-based violence, or sexist violence. How would the story have been reported today? The opening would have been different, the facts cited would have been different, the murder would have been seen as one in a long, sad list of women who died at the hands of men.

“The year has ended with another victim of sexist violence,” many journalists would have written.

But in 1995, the idea hadn’t made inroads, and without the concept, without the term, the reality didn’t properly exist. Language changes, and with it, our understanding of our present changes too. As does the production and the reproduction of reality. Things are as we say they are. Language is performative: It generates the world we live in. And in 1995, there was no gender-based violence. Instead this was a crime between brother and sister: sororicide. An isolated case. The perpetrator was Nicolás, not a *man*. The victim was Rosi, not a *woman*. She was alone with him: She wasn’t part of a sorry list of others like her. It was something inexplicable, and for that reason, nobody could accept it.

In 1995 the monster acted alone. Today we know there is a greater enemy, and that concrete instances of death and violence are the avatars of something much bigger, a far more dangerous aberration very difficult to eradicate. It doesn’t just end with a leap, with a suicide. It spreads like a virus and can only be seen and combatted if we name it. And that name, twenty years ago, didn’t exist in those newspapers. It was, instead, a quarrel between brother and sister. And the secret, the motive of their disagreement, was buried along with them.

THEN COMES THE most terrible part. You don't know who says it, but it echoes like thunder in the living room, announcing the coming of a storm.

They found Nicolás.

Dead.

Under a cliff.

The news tears you apart.

He jumped. His cousin found his body. He tried to hang himself first.

You listen to nothing that's said afterward. Because everything turns now into a sob. You don't shout, you don't speak, you don't know if you have words. Your eyes fill with tears. Everything blurs.

This is when María José hugs you and kisses your cheeks. You feel her body beside yours, you hug her tight, and you realize your tears are soaking into her hair. You feel her firm breasts pressing into you. And you can't avoid getting an erection.

Your world falls apart, and for a moment you wish this instant would last forever. The instant you dreamed of so many times. When you masturbate, or when you stretch out in bed and imagine what it would be like to be with her, kiss her, touch her, embrace her. The instant you imagined, it's here, just as the pain is searing you inside.

Your friend dead at the bottom of a cliff.

Your dick hard.

The world falling to pieces.

7

ALONG WITH THE photo of the cliff, there's another that burned itself into my mind. An incidental photo, a cliché, almost, situated at the bottom of the page in *La Verdad*: *A group of friends, family members, neighbors in front of the family's home.*

In it, my father appears, standing in the front, expression serious, arms crossed over his bulging belly, the pose very much his; it's a pose I had forgotten, and it stirred something inside me when I saw it. I also

identified some of the neighbors from the lowlands: my cousin Quique in the left corner, and my friend Juan Alberto to the right of my father. I was there too. I knew because I recognized the jacket. In the granular black-and-white, the details were all vague, but I was absolutely certain: That was my green jacket, and I was the one with my back turned, looking at the house with my hands in my pockets and talking with Juan Alberto.

I tried to remember when the photo was taken, but my memory was completely blank. I had thought I'd mapped out every single detail of that night and the day after, but it appeared this wasn't so. There were still empty spaces, and this seemed to be one of them. When was it? I'd assume not long after they found Nicolás's body. Juan Alberto was already back from El Cabezo. What were we doing there by the house? What were we waiting on?

There was something sinister in the image. I recognized almost everyone in it, and yet, they all struck me as strange. The scene came to me through the filter of the darkness of the crime, and the texture of the photocopy or scan seemed to project it further backward into time. It was like a relic from the forties, like something from *El Caso*, a scandal sheet popular long before I was born. An image that spoke of the heart of Spain, that benighted country that inhabits our collective consciousness and renews itself with every new murder, with every new disaster.

Time dissipated, and memory edged toward white and black. Twenty years was a century. The past century, in fact. A distance impossible to salvage.

"Look, it's Dad," I said the following Saturday to my brother Juan, showing him the pictures from the newspaper at El Yeguas.

I hadn't gone there since I'd returned from Ithaca, and they had invited me to lunch with other neighbors from the lowlands. Among them, I was surprised to see Garre for the first time since the funeral of my brother José Antonio's father-in-law.

"Hey kid, you still working on that book?" he asked after I showed the photo to my brother. "What is it, like the never-ending story?"

Juan ignored him and held the phone carefully in his hands like an antique portrait, touching the screen as carefully as if it were brittle photographic paper.

"Look at him," he said, and tears came to his eyes. He's always been the most courageous of us, but at the same time, the most emotional. *My Juanito's a little crybaby*, my mother used to always say.

"That's him, all right," José Antonio remarked. He was always the more even-keeled of the two. "That's his pose. Before the thrombosis, I mean. The way a man was in those days. Cards always close to his chest."

And that was true. That's how I remember my father too. Respectable, austere, well-mannered. He stood out for those reasons from other people in the village, and they respected him for it. He shaved twice a day, returned from work in the factory with his shirt clean, as if he'd been sitting in an office, and on the weekends, he'd throw on a tie before heading out to the bar. Juan Antonio was a gentleman, the neighbors said when he died. The dandy of the lowlands. This was why, when he had his stroke, lost his mobility, and had to start wearing a diaper, our world came crashing down on us. He never got used to it. We didn't either.

There, in the photo, he is still as he was. The rest of us had gone outside in whatever we had on. He had taken a few extra minutes to tie his tie. After all, it was December 25.

"Ay...," my brother Juan sighed. "He was the last one to catch on. I had to take him into a corner and explain what had happened. Even then, it was hard to get him to believe me."

"No one could believe it," Emilio said. "Rosario never was convinced."

"You can say that again," Juan interjected. "I had to change all the locks on her house and the bars on her windows."

"What?" I asked, surprised.

"You didn't know that?" Garre asked. "Hell, this bastard made a business of it. He got half the neighborhood to change their locks." He took a sip of his gin-and-tonic and turned to my brother. "Maybe you were the one who iced those two to make yourself a bit of coin?"

"Jesus, Garre," he protested. "You don't have any respect for anything."

I thought over what my brother had said and asked him what it felt like, going back to that house.

"It was one of the worst moments of my life," he responded. "I was all alone in Rosi's room, because Rosario was the only one there and she was busy fixing lunch. I had to go in Nicolás's room too. It was creepy! They were absolutely convinced someone had broken in. And meanwhile I couldn't stop thinking about what I'd seen there. The girl on the ground, covered in blood. A couple of times I had to walk outside to catch my breath, I made the excuse that I'd left behind some screws I needed."

"They were putting on a big show," Garre said again. "Changing the locks. They should have done that before. Put twenty locks on him. I know all about it. Fina's daughter, who used to live next door, told me everything. And then she heard their parents fighting. And more than once, their dad said to Rosario, *You knew, you knew what was happening and you looked the other way.*"

"Are you sure about that?" I asked.

"The neighbor told me, kid. I may not have gone to college, but I've got more wits than you have."

I didn't know if he was joking or being serious. There are people I've never learned to get. And I didn't get how anyone could ever find Garre's remarks funny.

"Sure, man," was all I managed to say.

"Don't lose the thread. I told you last time: Those two had something going on. And if they had changed the locks earlier, or if they'd told the investigators to look for him right away, it would have been a whole different story. Doing it afterward, though, what's the point? They frightened the whole damn neighborhood because of a lie."

III

THE CRIES OF THE PAST

YOU LEAVE THE house embarrassed. But you're fairly sure María José didn't notice.

Your father's in the doorway. He looks at you. Your brother. He looks at you. Everyone. They look at you. They don't know what to say. But you wouldn't know how to respond either.

It's all out in the open. There's nothing to do about it. Rosi's body is elsewhere now. So is Nicolás's. There's nothing more to wait for.

Why isn't anyone moving? Why are they all just standing there?

There won't be any more news. The worst has already happened. And yet, an invisible force anchors everyone to their place. This is where they have to be for now. All of them. The men and even the women now too. There's nothing to be afraid of anymore. The catastrophe has taken place. The movie's over. The danger has fled the driveway. The audience is all there, with nothing to do, nothing to stare at. Just themselves—and you—rooted to the ground, talking softly.

The Civil Guard takes statements from the neighbors. Someone points at you.

That's his friend, you hear them say.

An agent approaches.

Were you with him last night?

No, not last night.

Did you notice anything weird this week? Did he say anything unusual?

No, nothing unusual at all.

Thanks.

Those are all the questions he has. He doesn't write anything down in a little notebook. He doesn't bring out a pocket recorder. You get the sense it's not so much an interrogation as a formality. They have to ask, even if there's nothing anyone can say.

1

SINCE MY RETURN from Ithaca, I'd sunk so deep in this story that I'd barely spent any time with my wife. I hadn't realized it, but I had closed myself entirely to the world, with only one interest: writing. All day, but all night as well. After seeing those photographs and reading those newspaper articles, my nightmares had returned. Really, they'd never gone away, but those detailed words and those clear images of the past infused my memories with a new intensity. What had previously only been in my mind was now before my eyes as well.

I lay down seeing those things and tried to give them a narrative form. I needed distance from them, so I could treat them like sequences, dialogues, blocks of text. But I couldn't manage it, not entirely. The force of what had happened refused to let itself be tamed.

I've never felt any particular urgency when writing. As I composed my previous novels, I enjoyed each moment in front of the keyboard. I felt the pleasure of the text. With this novel, though, I found the story discomfiting. Writing wasn't exorcising demons, it was invoking them. Perhaps that's why I wrote so fast—why I'm writing so fast right now. To get to the end of it as soon as possible.

And yet, even as I told myself I needed to bring the book to a close, not wanting to live in it as I'd wanted to live in everything else I'd written, I needed a break. And at the end of July, I decided to stop and take a trip with Raquel. We agreed to spend a week relaxing at a hot spring in Alhama de Aragón that we had already visited one summer before. We needed time for ourselves. Time to disconnect completely. Reading, walks, good food, and sex. I owed it to Raquel. We owed it to each other.

The hotel there was in an old building from the late nineteenth century remodeled the year before. Being there, I couldn't help but see myself as a character in a fin-de-siècle novel from Central Europe, spending all day in a bathrobe, recovering from tuberculosis or some mental illness. And there was some truth to that, because I had gone there seeking a cure. Attempting to heal from the past. At least briefly.

I liked it for several reasons, but the main one was that I could bathe there without excessive fear of ridicule. Since childhood, I've had a complex about my body. More than once, I've said I was afraid of water when I was actually ashamed of stripping down. But at the spa, there was little pressure. There was flaccid skin there, swollen bellies, bodies in the twilight of life.... The thermal lake was tranquil, but I also had the feeling that my love handles, my stretch marks, and the hair on my back were in no way a violation of the canons of beauty.

I've been fat my whole life. I was fat in my childhood, but even fatter in adolescence, when I decided to start hiding beneath black T-shirts two sizes too large. In recent years, I've gotten over it, but that neurotic fat kid is still there, hiding somewhere inside me. The body's memory takes its toll, and it never goes fully away. It's there in your gestures, the way you move, the way you sit, the way you look at others, even the way you think about the world. There's a sense in which that trauma, that envy of healthy, strong, attractive bodies, permeates everything I write. It's the key to the frustration of Marcos, the timid adolescent in *Escape Attempt*, or the resentment of Martín, the professor in his forties in *The Instant of Danger*. In both novels, the protagonists are prisoners of their bodies. They perceive them as a burden they wish they could flee. In both novels, the main characters question a phrase uttered by Eusebio Poncela's character in the film *Martín (Hache)*. "No one fucks your mind," Marcos says and Martín writes. In both novels, it is my own fears and frustrations that are speaking.

At the spa, Raquel and I returned to the basics. Being together. Eating together. Walking together. Reading together. Just being. Time stopped and yet passed in the blink of an eye. I disconnected from Facebook and Twitter. I tried to put distance between myself and what I was writing.

But from time to time, as I was relaxing in the hot bath or floating gawkily in the thermal lake or walking beneath the trees, the past returned. Like an echo. Images, moments, ideas. I tried to let it go. I really did. But soon I gave up and decided it would be better to write it all down.

The spirits had traveled with me and even accompanied me into my dreams. One night, I woke paralyzed, with the feeling someone was pulling down the sheets. There was something in the room. That much I could perceive clearly. A presence I couldn't see, but could sense, even recognize. I don't know how to explain it. It was Nicolás. It was Rosi. It was the past. It was the feeling of discomfort, guilt, anxiety, and opaque silence that came upon me every time I went too deep into the story. A strange force tugging at the sheets.

I tried to move, but my body was stiff. I ground my teeth and struggled to scream. But my jaws seemed wired shut. At last I managed to shed my invisible shackles and emit a sound somewhere between a scream, a howl, and a sigh.

"What is it?" Raquel asked, shaking me awake.

"Nothing. A nightmare. Go back to sleep."

She did, but I couldn't. I turned on my phone and typed out everything I had felt. I could sense the viscous air of the world layered over what I wrote. It had been a dream, of course it had. But the sensation was real. It had sunken into my skin, and I couldn't shake it off. The effect remained with me for several days. Now, as I write, I invoke it again, and it makes me shiver. Rarely have I been so close to a force so complex.

We left the hot spring on a Monday morning. Along the way, we decided to stop in Belchite Viejo, the town

Franco had left in ruins as a testament to the brutality of the Republicans. In my book about Walter Benjamin and contemporary art, I had devoted a few pages to the Catalan artist Francesc Torres's works about that terrain of rubble, and I had wanted to visit it for a long time. Especially moving to me were his photos from the end of the nineteen-eighties, just after Terry Gilliam had filmed *The Adventures of Baron Munchausen* there, which showed the remains of the set alongside the vestiges of destruction. Two ruins interwoven. And two stages as well. Because conserving the town as a representation of barbarism was nothing more than turning it into a stage. And showing, as Francesc Torres had, the two ruins mingled in one space emphasized a notion of the world in which history, politics, and cinema are close collaborators.

By the time I arrived, the set pieces in Belchite Viejo had all been removed. But the town preserved the character of an image, a postcard, a theater stage of destruction.

Without intending to, we had arrived at the same time as a guided tour. What the girl describing the sights there told us left us frozen. The town was, in reality, a cemetery. Many of the bodies were interred in an enormous common grave, but the only people commemorated were the heroes of the fatherland, the national army. The other dead hadn't deserved to be named.

On our way back to Murcia, Raquel looked online for the special edition of the program *Cuarto Mileno* about Belchite, and we plugged her phone into the car speakers to listen. We heard the transcommunications of the falling bombs, the children singing in chorus, the paranormal events that researchers claimed occurred constantly in that area. They spoke of *perturbing energies* and *malign forces* that could be perceived as you walked through the streets and stepped into the shattered buildings.

I had noticed nothing like that. Nor had Raquel. We'd been led there by simple historical curiosity. What I did feel was unrelenting stupefaction, incredulity at the notion of what had happened there. It was inconceivable, unimaginable. And strangely, the sensation that reason had been outdone, that sense of the sublime and painful heart of tragedy, of the impossibility of approximating reality with words, was exactly what we all seemed to have felt when faced with the murder I was writing about.

Everything functioned as an image. The destroyed town reminded me of Roman ruins. Those ruins where the spirits of the past still dwell, the contemplation of which confounds logic because they bear witness to the immensity of historic time, beyond the particular time each of us inhabits. There is History, in capital letters, rising up over the concrete existence of men.

The sublime destruction of Belchite took me back, of course, to Caspar David Friedrich, as had the photo of two people staring over the immense cliff my friend had leaped from. Catastrophe as stage setting. Humanity faced with the abyss. Reason overwhelmed. That was how Francoism had handed down the story of the war. That was how the press described my friend's crime. A romantic tragedy.

A FEW MINUTES later, Juan Alberto arrives. In his car. With his father, the brother of Nicolás's mother. His father enters the house. Juan Alberto stays with you. He hugs you. You cry. He consoles you. For a moment, he holds back the tears. He says: My cousin, dude. My cousin.

Then he starts to cry. He, the toughest of all of them, a grown man, responsible. Now, he too is a kid.

You don't ask him what he's seen. You don't know how. You never will.

Moans are audible in the background. Outside, the silence crumbles.

You sit on the corner of the wall.

My cousin . . . my cousin . . . Shit.

That's all he says.

Fucking shit.

You're the one who responds.

Without blaming Nicolás. Without mentioning Rosi.

Nicolás was Juan Alberto's friend before he was yours. First cousins. The same age. You didn't meet him until he showed up in fifth grade at primary school. Him and all the others. After a bus that was taking them to

Sucina flipped on an embankment. You never talked to him about that. People got hurt, no one bad, though. But the parents decided it was better to change schools. And yours was the closest one. Now it occurs to you that if it hadn't been for the accident, you'd never have met Juan Alberto. You wouldn't be sitting with him on the wall. You wouldn't have shared your adolescence. He wouldn't have become your closest friend. The one you love most. And you would never have gone to El Cabezo de la Plata. Without him, that would be just another name and not much more. El Cabezo. The place Nicolás used to go on weekends. The big house on the other side of the mountain. The land dry and yellow. El Cabezo. Just a name, not much more.

But El Cabezo is a place. You've seen the cliffs. You've crossed the waterways. You've heard the hissing of the snakes. The call of the partridges.

It's the same for Juan Alberto when he comes to the lowlands. He, too, has walked the muddy streets. He's eaten mandarin oranges in the groves by the river. He's climbed the trees with you. Gotten grass stains on his sweatsuit. The lowlands, for him, are much more than a name.

You think about that for a moment.

The mountain and the lowlands, brought together, by chance.

The mountain and the lowlands.

And Nicolás jumping off a cliff.

2

ON MY RETURN from the spa, I turned to the novel once more. I needed to make the most of the weeks before September came and classes started and I had to attend to my responsibilities. As I wrote, shut up in my room with the blinds drawn and the air conditioner roaring, I kept going back to those books piled on the corner of my desk that served as inspiration for what I was trying to do. Capote, Piglia, Cercas, Delphine de Vigan . . . and especially Emmanuel Carrère. His works were those I consulted most, especially *The Adversary* and *My Life as a Russian Novel*, seduced by his peculiar way of telling things and the way he interwove the personal with the objects of his stories.

In those weeks, I sank into the pages of *The Kingdom*, the only novel of his I had put off reading, intimidated by its length and a plot that didn't strike me as especially attractive: the reconstruction of the origins of Christianity through two figures, Saint Paul and Saint Luke. When I started it, I soon realized my error. The book was a direct dialogue with the past I wished to reconstruct. In principle, Carrère's theme was the consolidation of a religion, but in fact he was speaking of his personal relationship with religion, and especially that moment in his life when he had embraced the Catholic faith and become a devout believer.

I recognized myself in those pages. Reading them took me back to the years when religion had been the central axis of my life. I had managed to get away from that quite some time before, but I can't understand my childhood and adolescence without the constant presence of the church. As with Carrère, religion was the center of my existence, but unlike him, I was never pious, I never had faith. For me, it was nothing more than a routine, inertia I had no idea how to escape. My years as an altar boy, weekly Mass, confession, the reading of the liturgy on Sundays, the *via crucis*, catechesis, meetings with the parish priest, visits to the monastery... Despite it all, I never truly believed. Why did I do it then? I've asked myself that many times, and I think I've finally found an answer. I did it for the same reason I've done so many things in my life: a sense of commitment. An acquired obligation I didn't know how to sidestep. Because it was what I was supposed to do at the time, and I didn't have the courage to refuse. I didn't want to disappoint my mother or my brother. And it was easier to go on doing it than to say no.

That's why I was an altar boy until I was fourteen, and I went to Mass every week until I was twenty-five, why I got confirmed, why I married in the church, and why even now, I still feel a pang of guilt when I hear the bells tolling on Sunday morning and I stay in bed at home. The church is inside me. The church and all it represents. Guilt, sin, prejudice. Some good things too. Charity, responsibility, sacrifice, piety. I suppose you never stop being a Christian, even if you stop believing, even if you never really did believe. It stays there forever, like a resident virus.

Funny enough, many of my memories of Nicolás come from then, from the time we spent together at church, and they come back to me more forcefully than my memories from school. The two of us alone in the sacristy, waiting for Father Antonio to arrive, altar boys petrified on either side of the cross, or ringing the bells before Mass, or preparing for our first communion and then, after confirmation, studying our readings and the responsorial psalmody, passing the collection plate, always watching each other out of the corner of our eyes, sometimes struggling not to giggle, last to take communion before the priest put away the chalice and eucharist in the tabernacle.

Like good Christians, we saw each other there every Sunday. And yet, we never had a single conversation about religion. And I can't say whether he had faith or whether, like me, he was pretending. Whether all that made sense to him or was an inherited obligation, something you just had to do, like brushing your teeth, combing your hair, or eating your rice with a fork instead of a spoon. Inertia, to be accepted to avoid provoking others' anger. Because Nicolás, like me, never defied his mother: He went on attending Mass every Sunday even after he was no longer an altar boy. Like me, he continued appearing in church to read the word of God. He ate of the body of Christ. Every week. Until the Sunday before the night when it all happened. Perhaps without believing. Or else thinking of heaven and hell. Still trusting in the forgiveness of sins, the resurrection of the flesh, and eternal life to follow.

Those years marked who I am. The years when I confessed my sins and wore black with a cross around my neck and the priests in Murcia would greet me in the street. The years when I even toyed with the idea of going to seminary. Luckily, I soon dropped that notion, realizing that I didn't believe enough in the dogmas, and much less in the institution, to devote my entire life to the church. But for a long time, I pretended that I did go to seminary and I nearly got ordained as a priest. I said this when I started working at a Catholic university, and I repeat it sometimes when I'm around atheist friends or those hostile to the church. I do this as a provocation and to make it known that I've transformed my life in recent years. But it's false. I never went to seminary. I never intended to be a priest. The grain of truth in this lie is that for some time, I studied the pipe organ at the seminary in Murcia. Those were my first years in college, when I was in love with sacred music and wanted to be an organist, like César Franck.

That strange obsession was born a few years before, in the music school a few Clarist nuns started in a small convent next to the chapel in the village. There Sister Francisca taught me solfège and piano, copied me several books of Baroque sheet music, and lent me dozens of CDs of Händel, Bach, and Pergolesi. There, too, the choir formed that I would play organ in for several years. We would practice several days a week, sing at weddings, communions, and church celebrations, and we even gave a few recitals in the city.

More than once, this nun's ill humor made our performances a nightmare of recriminations and groans, but still, in my heart, I found all that seductive. It made me feel important, and the music we played moved me. Bach's *Saint Matthew's Passion*, Vivaldi's *Gloria*, Gounod's *Sanctus*, Mozart's *Ave Verum*. I myself played Marcello's "Adagio," Bach's "Aria" from the *Suite Number 3 in D Major*, Massenet's "Meditation," and of course, César Franck, all simplified and adapted to the organ.

Often, the pianissimo of Pergolesi's *Stabat Mater* or the dissonance of Franck's "Panis Angelicus" would make the hairs on my neck stand on end. This was the closest I ever came to true faith. Like Cioran, I thought that "[m]usic is the final emanation of the universe, as God is the concluding emanation of music."

That was my religion. Not rock, not pop, not heavy metal. Not any of the music people my age listened to. Even in my teenage years, I was convinced that everything that came after Shostakovich was just noise and that the racket drilling into the eardrums of people my age was just a mishmash of coarse harmonies and frivolous rhythms repeating over and over with no appeal whatsoever. And so, when others filled their binders with photos of Axl Rose and Jim Morrison, I did it with sheet music of motets by Palestrina and pictures of the Merklin organ in the cathedral of Murcia. I couldn't stand going to bars where the music stung my ears, and like a bitter old man, I'd observe how today's youth were going to hell in a handbasket. And that is one of many reasons why I missed out on adolescence.

My tastes changed much later, when my doctoral dissertation was done and I was working as a professor at the university. That was when I opened up to life, to bars, to going out at night, to the music of my generation. As a man in his thirties, I discovered rock, pop, indie, EDM, all the music people enjoy when they're young. I subscribed to *Rockdelux* and stopped listening to Classical Radio. I turned the dial to Radio 3 and changed Purcell for New Order, Sibelius for The National, Jean-Baptiste Lully for Daft Punk, Tomás Luis de Victoria for Los Planetas. Instead of organ concerts at the cathedral, I went to modern music festivals in fairgrounds: SOS 4.8, Lemon Pop, FIB, B-SIDE, BBK, and Primavera Sound. I hung out with teenagers, traded my pleated pants for jeans, my loafers for New Balance sneakers, my dress shirts for checked T-shirts, my briefcase for a backpack. Youth came to me too late. I took the road backwards, lived backwards, put aside everything I'd become and tried to recover lost time.

But some things never come back, and time is one of them. And for that reason, I remain out of sync. I realize this still when I hear for the first time those bands that are already part of the memory of my contemporaries, when I lose myself dancing to "Blue Monday" or get excited on hearing Los Planetas, when nostalgia overwhelms me for what I would have felt if I'd known of all this in the right time, when I think of all that I missed, all the parties, all the concerts, all those moments I let pass, alone in my room, bitter at the world, listening to Naxos Music Group tapes of Corelli played live, posing as a misunderstood genius living in a world not up to his standards. I don't regret all of it. I am who I am thanks to that past. But sometimes I feel a bit of pity for that person.

IN THE BACKGROUND, the bells are tolling. It must be ten, time for Mass. Sometime later, the priest comes into the driveway. He greets you and comes inside. Not for long, just ten minutes. On his way out, he comes over and says, I need to talk to you. Let's take a walk.

Now?

Yes. We need to talk.

He guides you toward the tower, away from everyone else.

You need to walk, he says. Walking's good. It clears the head. I know how you feel. It's a hard time. I know you're angry. But don't let it eat you up. And above all else, don't blame God.

You look at him, unsure of what to say.

Don't blame Him, he repeats. Don't let this make you lose your faith.

My fucking faith, you think. What the hell does he know about your faith? He's hardly been two years in the village and he thinks he knows everything.

Call me Pedro, he told you when he arrived. Not Father.

A modern priest, your mother says. He plays *Super Mario Brothers* and he mentioned Sharon Stone in one of his sermons. He points to the faithful and tells them they're dead inside. That without God, they are nothing. He looks at the row of young women and warns them: Don't shut the door to your room to masturbate. The devil shows up when you're alone. You need your community. Your family. Because the family is what really matters. That's where God is.

He says these things in his sermons, in his religion classes at the high school. And he says the same thing to you now: You're not alone. Don't close yourself off to God. God is with you. Please, don't blame Him. Don't blame Nicolás. He was alone. It was the devil that did it. The demon. The demon forced him to do what he did. Don't blame God. Would you like to confess? Do you want God to forgive you for what you're thinking about right now?

Go fuck yourself. And tell God to do the same. To hell with him.

That's what you want to say. What you think in these moments. But you keep silent and look at the ground.

Pray, Miguel Ángel. Pray for him, but above all, pray for yourself. Don't blame God. Ask Him to be with you now. Don't question Him. Don't resent Him. God is love.

I'll pray, you say.

And you walk back out to the driveway.

3

I SPENT ALL of August writing. Some people wondered if I'd disappeared. I stopped going out at night, stopped making plans, and tried to disconnect from the world, even from those I was close to.

One afternoon, as I was shut away, I got a call from my old neighbor Julia. "Honey, I'm sick," she said with a quaking voice. "You said you were going to come see me during your break, and you don't even pick up the phone to call."

"Julia, I'm writing. I may not be working at the university, but I am at home, and I don't have a minute free."

"You're practically next door, you live five minutes away and don't come. All I want is to see you."

"I'll try to come by."

"You have time for everything you want, but when it comes to me, you're always busy. If you knew how much I cared about you, you'd make it a point to see me."

She was right. By chance, we'd wound up living in the same neighborhood, and I'd let too much time pass without calling her or going by. I knew that. She was a widow, she was almost ninety years old, and I was the closest thing to a son she'd ever had. And I felt similarly close to her. But I've never been much of a family person. Not with my mother, not with my brothers, and even with my friends, I've always kept my distance. I don't know if it's selfishness, or the need to live without explaining myself to anyone. Sometimes other people feel that I've abandoned them. Julia thinks that, of course. And she lets me know whenever she gets the chance.

"I'll come tomorrow, Julia, I promise."

"Don't lie to me like you always do."

I didn't, and the next afternoon I went to see her, and I sat on the patio for two hours doing nothing but talking. Or rather, listening to her complaints.

"The pain's eating me up, son. I can't take it anymore. And you don't even come to see me."

"Julia, I've got to finish the book I'm writing."

"The one about the two kids?"

I had told her about the novel on an earlier occasion.

"Yeah, the one about the kids."

"I won't see that one. I'll die before it comes out."

"Hush, Julia, don't be a doomsayer."

"I'm not well, boy, I can't hack it anymore. And even if you finish it, I won't be able to read it, I can hardly see nowadays."

"I'll read it to you."

Julia hadn't gone to school, but she'd kept track of all I'd written. She had every newspaper clipping that made mention of my books, and she'd read my novels word for word and even my doctoral dissertation. She used a prayer card of the Virgin Mary as a bookmark.

"So what are you writing in that new book of yours?" she asked. "Am I in it?"

"Yeah." I smiled.

"I can hardly talk right, though.... How's anyone going to understand me?"

"I'll figure out a way, Julia. You just tell me things and you'll see, everyone will understand."

"That was a bad thing, what happened, son," she said. "I've never been so scared in my life. What could have been going through Nicolás's head? A tragedy, a boy like that. Think how he must have suffered, running through the mountains, and finally jumping! I remember him well, you know. More than I do Rosi. And it hurts me so. And his mother, his mother too, poor Rosario. She died and she never did believe her son had done that. We used to talk together every morning, you remember?"

I nodded.

"And then that ugly thing happened and I didn't want to call her to come over, but one morning she told me she wanted to go out for a walk. She'd never been much of a talker, Rosario. And after all that happened, she talked even less."

"She never said anything about it later?"

"Never." Then she added after a moment's hesitation, "Well, there was this one time, I hadn't even asked her anything, and she said, 'My Nicolás, he was a very good boy. He didn't do what everyone says. Someone else killed my Rosi and they took my Nicolás away. They pushed him and pushed him, and he fell off a cliff. They killed my Nicolás is what they did.'"

"What did you say to her?"

"I told her she was right. And I said if that's what she believed, she could go talk to the police. And she said she had and they didn't pay her any mind, and that's why she had to change all the locks. I did it too, and I put lights in the backyard and the animals' pen."

"But it was obvious what really happened."

"I know, son, but the fear just got in my bones. And it never did go away. Not until I moved from the village to here. Here I feel like I've got more company."

I spent the whole afternoon with her, typing up everything she told me on my phone. Most of it I'd already heard before, had held on to, one way or another. Only one thing she said did I find shocking.

"He was a good boy, Nicolás. His aunt from Alquerías said so too. That same night, after dinner, he drove her to the village in his car, you know? And on the way, they came across this woman who tried to stop them. It must have been after midnight. And his aunt told him to be careful on the way back. He told her not to worry, that he was going to take a different road so he wouldn't come across her again."

"His aunt told you that?"

"She did. To show what a good, prudent boy he was."

The story struck me as odd, and I'd never heard it before. It didn't tell me much, but it did make me wonder. I was so deep in the novel that even the smallest unknown detail helped me interpret things. A girl alone on the way into the village hitchhiking at midnight. Might

Nicolás have gone back that way for her? Could he have let her into his car? Could that have anything to do with what happened afterward?

Probably not. Probably that information was useless, but when I heard Julia say it, I couldn't help but make conjectures. I doubted the police knew anything about it, and that was worth taking into consideration. Or maybe I'd seen too many movies and my imagination was getting the better of me. And one thing I took for granted was that I wasn't going to solve anything. My book wasn't a police investigation. I had already sensed that. There were facts, experiences, memories, and that was what I'd write down. I didn't need to interpret it all. And yet that image of a lone woman in the middle of the night remained in my mind for several days.

IN THE DRIVEWAY, you see cameras recording your neighbors. You recognize one of the journalists. Mateo Campuzano. He's on the news for Tele Murcia, you recognize.

They're vultures, someone says. They'll root around in everything. They've got no respect for our pain. They should leave people in peace. The bloodsuckers.

The journalist comes over to you.

Would you like to talk? They told us he was your friend.

No. I'd rather not.

Vultures, you think. They don't respect our pain.

It would be better if you talk, the man says, say something good about him, let people know what your friend was like.

You want to run away. But finally he convinces you, and you give in.

Look at my eyes, he says, not at the camera.

You're nervous. You don't even know what you're saying. You can hear your breath, halting, and can't control your words.

When it's over, you think to yourself: You betrayed Nicolás. You talked about him. In public. You can't imagine that twenty years later you'll write a novel and will have that same feeling again. Or that those images will come back to you and shatter you inside. You don't know—of course you don't know—that your tears and your cracking voice will be heard again years later. You don't know anything. Not yet. You're trembling. It's the first time you've ever been in front of a camera. And for the journalist—for everyone—you're the murderer's friend.

4

ON SEPTEMBER 1, I called the local offices of RTVE and asked to be connected to Cati Martínez.

"Of course I remember you," she responded after I told her who I was. "The video's been here on my desk waiting for you since December. I left it there the day I called you, and it hasn't gone anywhere. I thought you'd forgotten it or you no longer needed it."

"No, no, I do. I've been gone the whole time and now I'm finally ready for it."

"Come by whenever you wish. Monday after the midday news, for example. At four, if that works."

"I'll be there."

When I got in my car on one of the hottest days of the year—110 degrees outside, almost 120 inside my Citroën C4—I could sense that something important was about to happen. I drove slowly to the RTVE building, parked by the door, and got ready for whatever was to come.

Cati was waiting for me in her office.

"Here it is," she said, pointing at the tape. "It's the raw footage. Ten minutes total. Only two of them made it onto the news. Are you ready for it?"

From that moment forward, everything sped up. We walked into the viewing room, and the projection began.

"If you want, you can record it on your phone," she said, and I did.

I had imagined this would be the key moment of the novel—or at least one of them: me alone, in the viewing room at the TV station, confronting my past. But it wasn't like that. I had a journalist with me. I was looking at the screen through my cell phone camera. And the images just appeared, overlapped with everyday life. My cousin Maruja, Quique, the house, people on the street, Nicolás's body covered with plastic on a door serving as a makeshift stretcher, more declarations, my brother Juan...

"There you are," Cati said. She had remained silent up to then.

That was the only moment of intensity as I watched. My adolescent self, grieving as I spoke before the camera.

I had no time to analyze anything, to feel anything, though I knew my eyes were getting damp. I could look at the video again later. That eased my mind, and allowed me to make light of things.

"Jesus, I sure had hair back then, right?"

"You've changed, all right," the journalist said. "You look like a different person."

"Maybe I am."

Once we were done, I told Cati I'd like to document the scene. I didn't want to lose a single detail. I took photos of everything, even the label on the Betacam tape.

"You can keep it," she said.

"Thanks. I owe you a million gin-and-tonics and a million books."

"If you just finish what you've started, that'll be enough."

"You'll be in the novel."

"You probably tell everyone that."

"As a matter of fact, I do."

AFTER THE INTERVIEW, you don't know what to do. You go home, ready to hide in your room.

In the living room, you find your mother and Nena in the shadows, sitting across from each other at the table with the brasier at the bottom. Your mother is still in her nightgown, looking as sad as she has for days. You don't ask her why she didn't bother combing her hair, not today. Today, you need to be alone.

All this time, you've been surrounded by people. And with people around you, it's hard to think. Even in silence. You can only do it when no one's around. Like now. Lying in bed, face-up, trying to wake from the nightmare.

Nicolás...

His name comes to your lips. You say it to yourself, but it's as if you're talking to him, as if you were calling to him, summoning him.

Nicolás...

How many times has he been in your room? You have no idea. You used to read comics together, *Mortadelo and Filemón*, *Superlópez*, *Rompetechos*, *Zipi and Zape*, and *El botones Sacarino.* You recognized yourself in all of them. He was Mortadelo, he was Sacarino. You were Rompetechos, Filemón, sometimes Superlópez. The two of you were Zipi and Zape. Inseparable.

You would have liked your rooms to be connected. When he got a pair of walkie-talkies as a gift, you tried to use them to call each other, but the signal dropped out at three hundred feet. You learned Morse code and sent each other hard-to-decipher messages. You were far away but close, separate but together.

You set up the Atari 2600 and closed the door to play. Boxing, tennis, golf, Pac-Man, pinball.

That machine's going to drive you two crazy, your mother said.

You'd grab the ball and play basketball. He never missed a free throw. You only ever got it in when you were right under the basket.

Nicolás . . . you say now, stretched out in bed.

You evoke the life you spent with him.

Nicolás . . . you repeat aloud.

And you try, for the first time, to understand death.

5

WHEN I GOT home that night, Raquel had just crawled into bed. I was tired, but I knew I wouldn't be able to sleep. I shut my office door and uploaded the video to my computer. As I waited, I looked closely at the paper Cati had given me.

> **Title:** Current events. Brother-and-sister murder–suicide in Los Ramos.
> **Duration:** 00:08:35
> **Contents:** The murderer and suicide is N.P.L., and his deceased sister is R. 00:54:40 Shack with body covered with a sheet. 00:55:14 Road signs for Cañadas de San Pedro and Cabezo de la Plata. Village streets. Neighbors' declarations along with images of the village. 01:00:47 Statement of Miguel Ángel, close friend of the murderer. 01:02:40 End.

No one else in the neighborhood was named. Only me, *Miguel Ángel, close friend of the murderer.*

I stayed up all night staring at the film over and over, almost hypnotized, writing down what I felt, ideas...anything that passed through my mind.

I sat in front of the images and wrote, like the protagonist of my first novel. In *The Instant of Danger*, Martín wrote about things from the past, an immobile shadow projected onto a wall. I too found myself before the shadow of the past. And that was what left the deepest impression on me: my cousins, my brother, myself talking across time. More than the crime, more than the revelation of what had happened, more than seeing my friend's body covered with a plastic sheet and lying on a door balanced on two chairs.

I wrote down everything. I didn't know if I'd use any of it later, but writing it might be a way of putting history to paper, stopping it, exposing it in greater detail before my eyes. I was surprised by some of the things people said. Like my cousin Maruja, who lived at the top of the road that led to my house: "He never bothered anyone, he never talked bad about anyone. I mean, he didn't even talk to anyone. He'd come play basketball with the boys, and . . . He was just a really solitary guy. His family's solitary . . . That doesn't make them bad, they're not bad people. . . . It's just that they sort of keep to themselves."

My cousin Quique, one of Maruja's sons, appeared, then someone else from the neighborhood. All of them told the interviewer, *He was a great guy. I never noticed anything strange about him. No one could have suspected this.*

I imagined the scene from without. The remarks were all full of those cliches you hear on the news and no one ever fully believes. Then my brother Juan's face appeared and time jumped the rails. In 1995, he would have been more or less the same age I am now. And that took me twenty years into the future. I would be almost sixty, the same age as my brother. It was as though the door of time had just cracked before me, and the threshold led into a past that hadn't entirely vanished. The voices, the images brought it back, others and my own, which I observed as though it were one of history's echoes.

JOURNALIST: Were you supposed to go out?

ME: No, I mean, we were supposed to maybe do something, but just... we agreed we'd meet up, you know.

JOURNALIST: You never noticed anything strange about him?

ME: Nothing, no... Of the people... that I've known... One of the best. (My voice cuts out.)

JOURNALIST: You look very upset.

ME: I am, because... I can't really explain it. I don't know... I don't know, honestly.

JOURNALIST: You found out this morning?

ME: Yeah, at like five.

JOURNALIST: And as you said before, you're not aware that he drank or...

ME: Nothing. He doesn't drink, he doesn't smoke, nothing. He's someone who... he doesn't even like to get home late or anything. He's a homebody... studying... that's all.

JOURNALIST: Has he ever mentioned, or have you ever seen, any kind of anger toward his sister?

ME: Never. She was his sister. . . . I'd knock on her door and see if he was there. Is Nicolás home? Yeah, wait a minute, I'll get him. So, like . . . normal. Just a normal brother–sister relationship.

JOURNALIST: You're in the choir. I understand there's a day of mourning and the concert's been canceled.

ME: Yeah, we were going to sing this evening at seven in Sant Bartolomé, but under the circumstances, I don't see it happening. I don't think we're going to end up singing.

JOURNALIST: Thank you.

That babyface, those red eyes, that scraggly goatee, the tight skin, the bangs and the metal-rimmed glasses, that green hunting coat that looks modern now, vintage. And my way of talking. My Murcian accent, my insecurity, my timidity, my stutter. I'd hardly ever left the lowlands. The lemon trees in the background were still a part of my home. Lots of things have changed. But many more are still there.

Is there anything of this boy left in me? Maybe something in my appearance. The incipient goatee is now a beard. The bangs over the eyes are gone, as almost all the hair on my head is. The big, metal-framed glasses are now big, plastic-framed ones. Now, when I'm in front of a camera, I don't lisp and I'm not ashamed, or not as much as I was before. We may even weigh the same,

two-twenty, a little more. We have the same gestures, the same tired expression, the same sad eyes.

"You sure have changed," Cati said when she saw me onscreen. "You look like a different person."

Am I a different person?

Am I the same?

I still don't really know.

I went to bed sometime after three, and I couldn't sleep until the sun rose. I tossed and turned, and at one point I woke up Raquel.

"Is something up?"

"I saw the video. And I can't sleep. Everything's there. I'll show it to you tomorrow."

"Go on, get some sleep," she said, stroking my head like a child's and pulling it close to her chest.

And that was how I felt that night. Like a child. A spoiled child who had been torn to pieces.

I couldn't help linking that sensation with the images I'd watched that night over and over. Raquel didn't know it, but she was embracing two people just then, two times, two griefs. Because, without knowing really why, I started to cry.

Something broke loose inside me and I couldn't stop. I didn't know who I was crying for, my friend, his sister, the past, all those ghosts that had appeared before me, or if deep down it was for myself, for that me I had seen who still knew not a damn thing about life, that me who was sobbing because his friend had died and wasn't aware of everything that would come next, all the good and all the bad.

If time travel really existed, if you could journey into the past, if you could open a window and see everything, the sensation must be like what I experienced that night. Because that had happened: I had traveled into the past and seen myself. And to observe the past is to transform the present. Traveling in time always changes things. What I had seen had changed something inside me, I didn't really know what, and for a moment, I experienced the present as from a distance, and all the uncertainties of my world came crashing down before the uncertainty of myself in the past. The guilt, the anxiety, the insecurity...all of it took hold of me. I, who was so certain of everything, who had found a comfortable place that fit me, suddenly lost my footing. The me of before would never understand the thing that

I'd become. Was it right, what I was trying to do, what I was trying to write? I had asked myself those questions before, and though they had obsessed me, they had never upset me so. But that night, they came from a different time, crept into my body, and I didn't know how to shake them off.

YOU GET UP from the bed and you sit at the desk. You open a notebook, pick up a black pen, and try to write a word or two. You look for something that encapsulates your experience, that will capture the moment. But you are not yet a writer. And the words turn to lines and spirals crossing the paper: formless scribbles that tell you nothing.

You let your arm move on its own. It's not you who's drawing, it's your body. You don't turn the pages. Your hands do. You are elsewhere, far away, lost, not really sure how to come back.

And when you find yourself again in the real world, you tear the page out and throw it in the trash.

Twenty years later, when you're writing your novel, you'll remember this notebook full of scrawls and will think of it as the condensation of everything you felt. You will try to put it into words, and you'll be conscious of your failure.

You still don't know this, but you can sense it: Words always fail. Writing never gets to the bottom of things. With luck, it edges around it, grazes the wound. But the place itself always remains dark, opaque, indecipherable, like that scrawl you decide now to throw away.

6

THERE WAS A time when I thought that if I saw that video, the circle would close. I'd had the sense from the beginning that writing this novel would be a way of finding myself. And that my investigation would end when I stood face-to-face with my past. That was likely why I'd waited so long before going to the TV station. I knew that doing so might bring the story to an end. And in a way, it had been a culmination. But at the same time, something else had opened up there. Everything had become real. And what I'd told the journalist resounded in my head: *I can't really explain it. I don't know . . . I don't know, honestly.*

Twenty years later, I still can't explain it. Moved by uncertainty, I started to write this book. I'd thought talking with the Civil Guard might clear it up, or seeing the court papers, or the coroner's report, doing all the things my adolescent self—the one who hadn't known what to say or how to explain what had happened—would have wanted to do at the time. But now a year and a half had passed and all I'd done was talk to neighbors and visit archives. Repeating everything everyone already knew. What they said, what they saw, what they read. Recap the past, the trauma. Twenty years later.

Did I really want to know what had happened? Did I want to know why Nicolás killed his sister? How? What kind of resistance she put up? How long the struggle lasted? How many times he hit her? How long it took her to die? Did I want to know what it was like when he jumped off the cliff? How high it was? Did I want to know if his body was covered in bruises? How many bones he had broken? How long it took him to die? Did I want to know all that? And was there any point in knowing?

I know today that isn't the truth I was looking for. But back then, I wasn't sure. And the uncertainty awakened in me on looking back into the past made me believe that if I wanted to find answers to my questions, I'd have to keep looking, like a detective. And I had begun a novel, and one way or another, I needed to finish it. That commitment, more than any real need for knowledge, was what compelled me to look for the court records.

Everything was in the files: the police report, the coroner's remarks. That's what my friend Leo said. He was a writer, but a lawyer too, and knew how the system worked.

"Too bad I lost touch with my friend who worked in the courts," he said when I broached the possibility of looking for the files. "I haven't seen him in ages, and it doesn't feel right, calling him out of the blue just for this. But I'll catch up with him one day, and I'll bring this up."

"No worries," I said. "I'll try another approach."

That other approach was Luis Francisco, a Galician judge married to a neighbor from the lowlands. He had become a close family friend. He respected my father, and I knew he'd mourned him when he died.

I got his phone number from my niece, who had studied with his daughter and was still in touch with her. As the phone rang, I was still asking myself what approach I would take with him.

"Luis Francisco?"

"Yes, who's there?"

"Good afternoon, this is Miguel Ángel. Juan Antonio's son. From the lowlands. I'm José Antonio, Juan, and Emilio's brother." I listed all these names and details as though I were presenting him with my résumé.

"Ah, right," he responded after a moment.

I could sense his suspicion. Nobody calls with something to offer you anymore. The phone is there to ask favors or cause trouble, most of the time. And so I understood the mistrust in his tone. What could I be calling for after all this time?

He seemed to relax when I told him it was nothing urgent. "Everything's good, I'm working on a novel and I wanted to ask you a question about something related to it."

I described the project briefly and asked him whether I could consult the court records or I ought to forget about it. I asked in this way so he wouldn't realize right off that what I actually wanted was his help. This was a mistake because my phrasing implied that there was nothing to be done.

He told me he'd be happy to help, but getting hold of the files would be difficult. Much time had passed, and they'd likely have been sent to the archives in Zaragoza or Madrid. I didn't have a strong justification for examining, because I hadn't been part of the case. And they wouldn't put a public servant to work looking around for several days just because some novelist was seeking information. The prospects weren't good.

But since the murderer had died and there was no trial, the court filings would contain no information that wasn't in the police report.

"If you know anyone in the Civil Guard," he said, "ask them for a favor. That's your only sure bet."

"I will," I said. "Thanks anyway."

I assumed that he was trying to dodge my request. Later, Leo told me that he'd probably have tried to solicit the court report if I'd insisted. But he was a judge, and that was a legal gray zone. And so he had done no more than I'd requested. And that was fair.

"At any rate," he said before sending my family his regards and hanging up, "it's pretty obvious what happened there."

I didn't respond, and soon he went on: "He must have been abusing her. They may even have been in some kind of relationship. These things happen in small towns, in isolated areas. I'd figure he got jealous that night. And he just couldn't bear it anymore."

"Yeah, that's sure what it seems like," I responded more or less firmly, as if I too had come to that conclusion.

When the call was over, I thought of how coldly he had explained the details of the case and his blunt approach to the events. That was the first time an authority had spoken of a sexual motive. I'd heard Garre say it, and some neighbors too. It was always present somewhere in the conversation, spoken or silent, casting a shadow, a black hole around which all speculation revolved. And my entire life, I had tried to avoid these speculations.

Had Nicolás tried to rape Rosi? Had he done it before? Did they have some sort of sexual relationship? One of my initial fears when I began the book was that I would have to confront these questions sooner or later. I had plugged my ears to keep from hearing the innuendo and unfounded rumors. I had tried to ignore the gossip of Garre and the other neighbors. But the judge had been conclusive, unequivocal, and his words struck at the wall I'd been building to avoid thinking about all that. That same afternoon, I found myself taking seriously for the first time the possibility that Nicolás had tried to rape his sister. I realized that this intimation wasn't a new one for me—in some way, it had been there all that time, lying in wait, but I had resisted formulating it clearly. My reaction to the judge's thoughts—*Yeah, that's sure what it seems like*—was less a hint to him that I agreed than a response to my own unconscious.

Nicolás tried to rape Rosi.

When I wrote those words in the draft file for my novel, I felt a pricking in my stomach. I had just betrayed my friend. I was unveiling something I had promised to omit until I was absolutely sure, until I had proof. I had begun my project setting aside my thoughts about everything that had happened, giving others a voice and silencing my own. But that afternoon, this thought came to me, and it would have been dishonest not to record it. I didn't really admit it to myself. My fingers pressed the keys softly, as though in a whisper, ashamed at yielding before hearsay.

The words of the judge had forced me to become a judge myself, to take a position, to break that distance from the murder I had struggled to maintain from the beginning. Because to write down, to think, that Nicolás had raped Rosi introduced another element into the equation: He was now no longer just my friend, the murderer, but also my friend, the rapist. And for some reason, writing *rapist* hurt more—still hurts more—than writing *murderer*. Maybe because to write *rapist* takes us into the quicksand, an atrocious place of violent perversity that touches on the nature of sex and pleasure. And those questions, in regard to Nicolás, remain unimaginable for me.

Hard as it is to believe, he and I never talked about sex. It was taboo. I could clearly sense his discomfort every time someone appeared naked in a film, or kissed, or there was any kind of sexual encounter. He would look down, and I'd do the same. I assumed it was what I was supposed to do. Proper. Looking away. Sex was something dirty. A private perversion we couldn't share.

When I think of my sexuality then, that filth comes back to me. I remember shutting myself up in the bathroom to masturbate with my brother Emilio's porno magazines, thinking about movie actresses, television presenters, classmates, girls from choir, nuns from the convent, my cousins, my neighbors, my sisters-in-law, all the women I could compose an image of in my mind. I probably even masturbated thinking about Nicolás's sister.

I remember the viscosity of it. I remember the guilt and tears. That was my most horrible secret. The shadowy being that lived inside me.

Those were my darkest years, years of unhealthy desires, of touching the border of something pernicious, of contained energy always on the verge of exploding. I suppose that's why imagining Nicolás raping Rosi still unsettles me in a way I can't easily cope with. It means, somehow, reliving that closed world of solitary sin, full of immoral fantasies and degenerate visions. It means suspecting that the twisted motive that may have led Nicolás to abuse his sister abided within me as well. Could I have done what he did? I wanted to believe I couldn't. But I confess that sometimes, I think that repressed sexuality, full of guilt and remorse and impiety, might have led me to do terrible things. And the mere notion of such a possibility fills me with dread.

I spent the entire afternoon absorbed in these ideas. The only way to stop thinking about them, I sensed, was to find the case files. In them I hoped to find some kind of answer.

The next day, as soon as I got up, I called my brother Juan. I remembered he had mentioned his friend in the Civil Guard a time or two.

"Yeah, Inspector Jiménez," he said. "He was one of the guys assigned to the case. But we weren't friends. Larry brought him to lunch at El Yeguas once, and that's where we met. I don't think those two are in touch anymore, though."

Larry—Hilario—was the bar owners' cousin and a childhood friend of my brothers. They had grown up together, and he was like a part of the family.

"If you see him, ask him, please," I said.

"I'll tell Emilio, he runs into him some evenings. But only if you come to lunch on Saturday. You've been a stranger all summer."

"Sure," I agreed. "We can celebrate my saint's day, it's right around the corner."

NIGHT COMES, AND you don't know how you'll fall asleep. You close your eyes, and the day's memories flood your mind. You toss and turn in bed. The images won't go away. Rosi's body. The interview. Nicolás jumping over a cliff. You take a deep breath and try to call up something happy from your past. And then María José returns. You imagine her holding you, feel again her breasts pressing into your body, and for a few minutes, this stops the flow of thoughts.

You feel yourself getting hard, and you slip your hand under the sheets. You grab your dick tight and start to jerk it.

María José . . . you say softly, in the same tone you used before to utter Nicolás's name.

María José . . . you whisper again as you lower your underpants and push the comforter aside.

María José . . . you repeat in the darkness, the scene of her holding you elaborating into something more.

But you hardly have time to fantasize about her body. You feel an explosion of pleasure, and semen splashes your belly.

That pleasure turns immediately to pain, and tears flow with your semen.

What have you done? Do you respect nothing anymore?

You wipe yourself off with the crusty sock you keep in the back of the drawer, and you can't help but feel guilty.

You've befouled Nicolás's memory. Instead of praying, you have fallen into sin. You're sick. You deserve to throw yourself off a cliff. For what you've done now, for all the other things you've done.

You repent.

You cry.

For now and for all the other times.

You repent for the obscene monster inside you that you wish you could eradicate. The being you hide, but that you know exists. Because no one knows of that abomination. Not even Nicolás. Only once did you show him a dirty magazine. And he looked the other way. You knew then that you couldn't talk with him about those things. He was upright. A good Christian who knew how to control his impulses. Not like you, who falls, over and over, who sins day after day. Despite appearances, despite the cross worn around your neck, despite your presence at Sunday Mass and your belief that God is watching you from above. You are a monster. That night, especially. Filthy, doomed, empty, dark, impure.

You repent.

You pray before falling asleep.
For Nicolás.
For Rosi.
For yourself.

7

WHEN I SHOWED up at El Yeguas on Saturday morning, my brothers weren't yet there. As I waited, I ordered a coffee to wake myself up and settled in at one corner of the bar, not wanting to be seen by the other customers. I had been there many times, but I still felt defenseless without my brothers, uncomfortable, out of place. Abellán must have sensed this when I greeted him upon entering.

"How's the book going?" he asked as he sat next to me.

I was surprised he was speaking to me. I hadn't forgotten what he had said to me one of the first mornings when the topic of Nicolás had come up at the bar: *Don't go stirring up shit.* He seemed to remember it too.

"Don't take me wrong," he said after I told him the book was moving along well, but slowly. "It's just all that was so awful. It was a bad time for all of us. We're lucky the Civil Guard took over the case and not the local police. I wouldn't have been able to take it."

"I imagine."

"You know, I took his father to gather the last bits of evidence. He was convinced someone had broken into the house. I conveyed that to my colleagues, but they dismissed that outright. There's no room for doubt, they said. His pants were covered in blood. Her blood. He'd beaten her with a weight. Until he'd killed her. And then there was . . . well, you know. The other thing. That."

"What?" I asked.

"Well, he forced her. That much is obvious."

"Yeah. Obvious."

"Her maxi pad," he added. "A maxi pad, with wings, those things don't just fall out of a pair of panties. And they said it was on the ground. So he'd forced her, no doubt about it."

I didn't know how to react, and I took a sip of my coffee with milk, which I had just set down on the bar. It burned my tongue and throat and my eyes filled with tears. Abellán was staring at me. He must have known his words had struck me deep.

"I mean, that's all conjecture," he went on. "I'm not communicating that in any official capacity. It's just what I was told. But you know, they closed the case. There was no need to really go digging around. They had their motive, most likely. And what was evident was that he was the killer. There are too many other things going on in the world to waste time on the details of something that's dead and buried."

"Sure," I conceded.

Abellán added, "Now what was I supposed to tell their father? Nothing of what my colleagues had told me, obviously. So I said they'd go on investigating until all the other avenues had been exhausted. You know, sometimes it's better just to lie."

I nodded.

"But lies can be dangerous, and as I was taking him home, he told me there were some concrete blocks in the yard next door and he thought that was probably where they'd climbed onto his property. If the Civil Guard was going to keep investigating, they'd have to look into that. And when we got to the lowlands, I knocked on Fina's door and asked if I could go out there. And it was true there was a pile of blocks along the wall between the two houses, and a person could have climbed over them and jumped to the other side. But to do that, they'd have had to climb the wall onto Fina's property first. And anyway, the blocks were covered in cobwebs. They hadn't been moved in years. It's not like they were stacked up so someone could climb over. And I told their father that. But I couldn't manage to convince him. No one ever did. Not the mother either. It's easier to close your eyes than face the truth."

When my brothers arrived, they were surprised to see me there talking to Abellán. I finished my coffee, thanked him for his sincerity, and sat down at the table with them. As they brought out our lunch—snoots, bacon, blood sausage—I noted down the details of the conversation I'd just had.

"I talked to Larry," my brother Emilio remarked. "He says it's been forever since he's seen the guy from the Civil Guard. He left Murcia and they stationed him elsewhere. And he doesn't have his new number."

"Well, at least he tried," I responded.

For days I thought about other possibilities I could explore, but class had started, and little by little, the university bureaucracy was devouring me. Department meetings, faculty meetings, education quality assessments, advisory sessions for thesis papers, dissertation panels, my own classes in art theory . . . all this took away the time and energy writing demanded, and with the weight of weeks, the novel ground to a halt. Sloth took hold of me, and the need to know faded away, almost to nothing, and it might have done so had I not received a call the last Thursday of October just after leaving class.

"Come to El Yeguas tomorrow," my brother Emilio said. "Larry found Inspector Jiménez."

IV

PERFORMANCE

YOU WAKE UP. Tuesday, December 26.

You don't shower. You dress in the same clothes as yesterday. The same clothes you've worn all week. The blue shirt with the sagging neckline, the same green jacket.

You have breakfast at the table with the brazier in the bottom, still warm from the night before. Nena knows how to stir the embers so they stay hot until midmorning. She raised your mother, and she's been there half a century, in the same place, looking out the window day after day, without uttering a word. But today, she decides to talk.

"Those young 'uns are all crazy. It runs in the family."

Then she looks out the window and falls silent as a stone statue.

You say nothing. You wolf down your milk and cookies and go outside. You walk down the street. Your home, the home of your brother Juan, the home of your brother Emilio, the home of your cousin Maruja. All are empty. All are silent.

The people are out in the driveway. The noise is coming from there. Everyone's waiting for the vigil. But the coffins haven't arrived. The event they're waiting for hasn't yet begun.

Julia's there, your mother is there, the neighbors are there. María José isn't there.

She's gone back to Murcia, her grandmother says before you can speak.

You breathe a sigh of relief. At least you don't have to confront the shame again, the guilt, the regret. But the relief is bittersweet. Because you do want to see her, in your heart you yearn to play the role of the devastated friend. There is no distance, the world is closer to you.

1

I SPENT THE day preparing my interview with the Civil Guard. When I got in the car to drive to El Yeguas, I was more aware than ever of the artificial nature of what was about to take place: At last, the investigator finds the person who was at the scene of the crime, and he tells him all he knows. I had seen that scene a thousand times in the movies. I had read it in all too many novels. And it was about to happen in real life. A life cut through by literature.

When I look at it now from a distance, I think I had stopped caring by then what Nicolás did to his sister. What fascinated me was seeing myself as a character in a novel, writing the reality of my actions and guiding myself toward the search for truth. It was then, I believe, that the banal performance began that brought everything to ruin.

I reached the bar a little after eight in the evening. I was surprised to find it closed. The lights were on inside and I peeked into one of the windows. Antolín was setting up the tables. When he saw me, he stopped what he was doing, opened the door, and invited me inside to wait.

"We open for dinner on Fridays, but people don't come till later," he said, serving me a beer before I'd even ordered.

It was the first time I had seen El Yeguas empty. Strangely, I found myself thinking of it as a film set waiting on the cast and crew, a bare stage before the actors make their entrance.

The first person to arrive was my brother. Larry had needed to stop at the Civil Guard station and would be a little longer. Each second's delay was like something from a novel. Reality was taking its time before breaking into fiction; the world was swelling with narrative tension.

Larry arrived forty minutes after the agreed-upon hour with the Civil Guard in tow.

As he walked toward us, I couldn't help but compare him with detectives I'd seen in movies. Five o' clock shadow, hair dirty and yellowish, worn-out brown leather jacket... Mentally, I noted down all the attributes of this dark, tormented character. What plucked me from the world of fiction was the white canvas bag hanging from one of his shoulders.

"Jiménez," Emilio said. "It's been centuries since I've seen you. Hey, this is my brother."

The Civil Guard shook my hand firmly, but otherwise paid me little attention. As if I didn't exist, he turned to my brother and asked him what he'd been up to.

"Jack shit. Jack shit is what I've been doing. At this point, I'm just waiting to get old and collect my social security," Emilio said, trying to make light of things, not really succeeding. "Five years of nothing, riding my bike to El Yeguas so I won't spend money on gas."

"After all we've done, right, Emilín," Larry said. Larry had a job, at least, but he'd had to trade in his Audi A6 for a secondhand Ford Escort that he sometimes parked far away so the people at the bar wouldn't see it.

They drank a few beers and went out to smoke on the small patio by the coal oven, which was ready for dinnertime. I followed them, beer in hand.

They spent half an hour asking about each other's friends and children, politics, and Real Madrid. I started to get the sense that Jiménez had come to El Yeguas to discuss a past quite different from the one I wished to talk about. But then we sat down for dinner, and after a few minutes, Jiménez looked at me for the first time, and he said, "So, what did you want to know? Shoot."

I'd been trying to figure out how to bring it up mid-conversation. Now I breathed a sigh of relief. I told him I was writing a novel, that I needed to see the case files, and that I was hoping to talk to him about his experience, since he'd seen everything firsthand.

"Well, that's what we assume," he responded. "Can you remind me which case this was?"

"Brother and sister. Christmas Eve, 1995. He killed her and then he killed himself."

"How? Sitting in the car in the garage?"

"No, he jumped off a cliff."

"You sure you don't mean the guy who cut the girl's throat and then jumped off a balcony?"

"No, no. Definitely not."

I looked in my phone for the photo of the article in *La Verdad* and showed it to him.

"Ah, yeah, I think I remember," he said, not sounding convinced. "I think so. I think I was there that day. I'd have to look."

"Dammit, Jiménez, of course you were there," Larry said. "We talked about this. You've got a memory like a fucking sieve."

"All right, shit," Jiménez replied. "You can't imagine the bullshit we have to see. Anyhow . . . ," He turned to me. "If the file's there, I'll find it for you, I don't see any problem with you having a look. You're not supposed to, but there's lots of things you're not supposed to do, and in the end people wind up doing them. . . ."

"I really appreciate it. You can't imagine what a help that would be."

I said that to bring the conversation to a close. I had the feeling he wasn't comfortable. He had gone there looking for something else—a reunion with an old friend—and I didn't want to stand in the way.

We had grilled ribs for dinner, and fried potatoes with garlic and parsley. Larry ordered bottle after bottle of white wine. He knew the distributor and had worked out a deal between them and the bar's owner. The conversation jumped from one subject to another, but nothing about the case, as if Jiménez were consciously ignoring it. But then, as I was refilling my glass, he asked me, "So, do you think you can deal with looking at the photos in the file and everything that's in it?"

"Honestly, I don't know," I responded after a moment's hesitation.

"The photos will probably be in black and white, because back then, we only developed them in color if there was a trial. Still, they're not going to be pretty. And if you say it was your friend…"

"I know. I've got to do it, though."

Then I asked him if a person ever got used to stuff like that.

"No one does. There are times when I struggle to get to sleep. Especially if there are kids involved."

And he told us that in the cases where he was a lead officer, he tried to attend the autopsies.

"I do it because I want to learn all I can, and the body tells you everything. And afterward, I go out and eat until I'm ready to explode. What's the explanation…? I don't know, I've asked psychologists and my colleagues and no one's given me an answer."

"I guess it's the connection with life," I replied. "Maybe after seeing the most animal part of us in death, pure biology, you need to feel that biology in action. Feel that you're alive, move your organism from within. I don't know, that just occurred to me."

Jiménez turned thoughtful for a moment, refilled his glass, and changed the subject without responding or looking at me.

At midnight, the bar started emptying out, and soon it was just the four of us at the table with a bottle of White Label between us. I didn't have anything to do the next day, but I didn't know how I'd get home with all the alcohol I'd drunk. My body couldn't take anymore. When my brother said it was time to go, I stood and had to grab my chair to keep from falling.

Larry and Jiménez stayed a while longer.

"We need to catch up," Larry said ironically, looking at the bottle of whiskey.

"I'll try and find that file as soon as I can," Jiménez said. "But I'm pretty busy the next few weeks. I guess you all heard: On Monday the guy who killed his kids in Santomera is getting out, and we need to be on the alert."

"I saw that on the news," my brother said.

I had seen it too. Fifteen years had passed since he strangled his two children with his cellphone cable. Now his sentence was over.

Without really thinking, I asked Jiménez, "If my friend hadn't killed himself, how long would he have gotten?"

"I don't know," he answered, "but he'd probably be out by now. For sure. Look at that, that's something for your novel right there."

I grinned. I said goodbye to them all, giving my brother a kiss on the cheek and shaking the other two men's hands.

I got in my car with those final words resounding in my head. As I returned home, leaning forward onto the steering wheel, eyes blurry, knowing I should have called a cab, I kept thinking about what would have happened if Nicolás had gone to jail and served his sentence and now he was back home. If I could only still remember him as a friend because I'd never had to look him in the face knowing what he was capable of.

That night was the first time I asked myself what his life would have been like if he'd accepted what he'd done, and what he'd be like now, after twenty years had passed, returning home or moving elsewhere and getting back in touch with his friends. It would have been a different story, obviously. And I'm not sure if I'd have known how to tell it. That was also the first time it occurred to me that maybe it was better that Nicolás was dead. Not just for him, but selfishly, for the rest of us. For all of us who had been there and would have struggled to look in the eyes of that monster we had once loved.

THERE THEY ARE, someone says.

The two of them? They're holding a vigil for the murderer too?

Two hearses bring silence with them. Everyone stands aside. The vehicles come closer and park next to the house. Brothers and parents gather to receive them.

My Rosi! My Nicolás! their mother cries.

The brothers say nothing. The father looks at the ground.

Two coffins. Two closed caskets.

In their wooden boxes, they are equal. Victim and murderer. They are her children. Him and her.

My Rosi! My Nicolás!

Her only daughter, her youngest son.

Two wooden boxes, their contents concealed. An enigma. Who is who? Where is Nicolás? Where's he hiding? What's he playing at? You can't avoid this thought arising in your head.

A game.

A closed box with dominos inside. Nicolás has several. Left over from when his house was the village bar.

Glasses, dominos, and decks of cards. The cold smile, the bluff, the indecipherable gaze.

Maybe he was more there than anywhere else. It's there that the frozen image your mind preserves comes from. Pausing, looking, meditating, sidetracking you with his smile, playing at not telling.

A game. Always a game. An enigma. Never to be unraveled. Like now. More than ever. Nicolás, bluffing. And you falling into his trap. Not knowing which dominos he had. Not knowing which box contains his body.

2

A FEW DAYS after I met Jiménez at El Yeguas, I traveled to a literary festival in Toronto where I had to read fragments from my first novel, which had just been translated into English. It was the first time I'd attended, and for a week, I tried to forget Rosi and Nicolás. I didn't write, I didn't think about the book, but the story didn't go entirely away. Every time someone asked me what I was writing next, I responded in English, "a nonfiction novel about a true crime in my youth." And with these words, I felt the novel was still there with me.

I returned to Murcia on All Saints Day, to visit my parents' tomb. It's the one time of year I go up to the cemetery—I say *up* because it's built on a hill outside the village. The year before, when I was in Ithaca, my brothers were the ones who cleaned and left flowers at their graves. This year, despite my weariness and jet lag, I felt obliged to. I even wanted to, more than ever. With the novel in my head, I had the sense that the day would be different, that whatever happened there would become a subject for me, that everything that now occurred might have a place in this story.

As I walked up the steep road to the cemetery, I kept thinking that I'd eventually pass my friend and his sister's tomb. I'd never had the courage to visit them. Every first of November—and a few other times, when I'd gone there for funerals—I had intentionally avoided them. That afternoon, I wouldn't. I'd been thinking it over all morning. I was certain of my intentions. On the flight from Toronto, I'd even envisioned it in my head.

A long street divides the cemetery in two parts. My family's tomb is on the right, my friend's family's on the left, a few rows further down. As I walked, I saw his brothers, his aunts and uncles, and his cousins, standing absorbed before the tomb. I thought I might walk over and greet them. I almost did. But at the last second, I didn't dare. I bowed my head and hurried toward my parents' graves, assuming Nicolás's family would be gone when it was time for me to go.

My brothers had already arrived, and were conversing calmly, sitting in the folding wooden chairs that we kept stored inside the monument. I gave them each a kiss on the cheek, then stood a few silent seconds before my parents' crypts. There was a time when I could hardly do it without my eyes filling with tears. But everything has grown cold with time. Now the photos of my parents on the marble plates bring only a bitter smirk to my lips. And their four sons' presence, talking of this and that, repeating old stories, is theatrics, a reproduction of something that once was and will never be again.

As usual, I imagined that afternoon that the four of us seated before the mausoleum were having a conversation such as might follow a meal, and our parents were there, listening closely from where their photos stood. I told my brothers all about Toronto and said the jet lag had kept me up all night. In my heart, I was telling this story to my parents, especially my mother, whom I called every time I returned from a trip. I still remember the vertigo I felt the first time I could no longer do so. I couldn't tell her I'd arrived in Oslo, I couldn't tell her I'd made it home. I was so used to it, I seem to remember, that I even dialed her number without realizing it.

We stayed by the tomb until the sun started to set and the cold wind from the mountains chilled our bones.

"I need to go get my wife, she's at her parents' grave," José Antonio said, folding his chair.

Emilio and Juan got up and folded theirs in turn.

"I'm going to stick around a little longer," I said. "I'll lock up and blow out the candles."

I needed that excuse to stay behind so I might visit Nicolás's grave in peace. I waited a few minutes, put the chairs inside the tomb, and snuffed the candles so the flowers wouldn't burn. I locked the door and crossed myself reflexively. I hadn't been to Mass in years, but certain gestures from my Catholic days were like tics that wouldn't go away.

"Till next year," I murmured, not really sure what I was saying.

I crossed the street that divided the cemetery and walked down toward my friend's tomb, hoping there would be no one there. But when I arrived, I saw his brothers hadn't left. It was too late to turn back now, and if I walked past, they would see me. The younger one looked over. The older one nodded slightly in greeting. And at that moment, it all came crashing down. The unease I had felt a year and a half before, when our eyes crossed on the feast day of the Virgin of the Lowlands, returned with unusual force. What was I doing there? My friend's family, ignorant of my writing, was concentrated on their private grief, which my book might invade like an intruder. How would I feel if someone were to write about my parents? How much of our lives belong to others? Who are others, really? Friends? Family? What right do we have over them and their memory?

My friend had died. My friend had killed. Something of the suffering around that formed a part of me. And it was that suffering that I was writing about. That was what I told myself then, when those questions surfaced violently inside me. That was how I tried to justify myself. But I didn't manage to, not entirely. My suffering and theirs were incompatible. If I could speak, if, with the passage of time, I could write what I am writing right now, it was because there was something that hurt me less than it hurt them. My life hadn't been shattered irrevocably; theirs almost certainly had.

When I saw them at the mausoleum like statues, not talking, not looking each other in the eyes, I sensed that their wounds would never heal. And when I returned home that afternoon, I still couldn't say whether there was a need to write all that down. I opened the journal where I sketched out my ideas and only managed to scrawl out a single phrase: *Write... why?*

DON'T GO IN, Miguel.

Your mother says that. Julia says it. Your cousin Maruja says it too.

Don't go in there. It's not pretty.

This time, you listen. You don't go inside. Resting on the wall, leaning on the door, sitting on the ground, offstage, but inevitably hearing what's going on inside. Because the walls can't contain the lamentations.

That house is like the hollow body of an instrument.

Ay, my Rosi, why did you kill her?

Ay, my Nicolás, what did you do?

You were such a good girl...

You were such a good boy...

Their mother's voice is the only clear one. Rosario. All else is weeping, shrieking, impossible-to-identify groans. Rosario's voice sticks in your head.

Why did you kill my Rosi?

Why did you take my Nicolás away?

You imagine what's going on inside. You reconstruct it through the words of the neighbors walking out.

They've laid them in the living room. One next to the other. With a photo on top of each coffin. They didn't open the coffins. The bodies, they say, are in an awful state.

Their mother won't stop crying, kneeling on the ground, arms open, one hand touching each of her children.

Rosario . . . poor woman.

Their mother . . . their mother . . . is the neighbors' lone lament.

Their father is still outside, leaning on the door, same as the day before. The neighbors approach and greet him in a whisper. They try to console him. He looks at them. He says, *Thanks* and invites them in. But he doesn't accompany them, he leans against the wall, staring just as he did that first night.

Your eyes cross at some point. He looks at you, but you don't know if he sees you. You look into his stare. In it, you see the void. The most radical nothingness. Not a single recognizable sign of humanity. His are the eyes of an object. A stone. Pure minerality. You have the feeling those eyes will never look again. Death has entered them, like a virus. And it will never abandon them.

3

MORE THAN A month and a half after our meeting, Inspector Jiménez had given no sign of himself. I wrote unanswered emails, made unanswered calls, and finally pressed my brother to ask Larry if he knew anything.

"He's been busy," Emilio told me on the phone a few days later. "He told Larry to tell you to prepare yourself in case it can't be done. Apparently, it's more difficult than he thought."

He had told me nothing was impossible. But this seemed to be. I'd have to wait. There was no other option. At least, that's what I thought. But then, once more, fate worked in my favor. That same week, a friend of mine won a literary prize, and that was when I met Vicente.

Diego Sánchez Aguilar won the Setenil Prize with his first book of stories, and Leo and I decided to go to the award ceremony at city hall in Molina de Segura. We got there toward the end, when some of the attendees were heading to a bar next door for beers. We joined Diego and his wife, the jury, several writers from Murcia, and some friends who had also come alone.

At the bar, Leo said hi to a guy with long hair I didn't know and spoke with him for a few minutes. Then the two of them walked over, and Leo introduced us.

"Remember I told you I knew someone who could help you with the court documents. This is the guy: Vicente."

I said hello and stared briefly at the long gray hair falling over his shoulders and his faded Iron Maiden T-shirt, which was fraying at the cuffs. He looked like anything but an officer of the court. He and Leo had worked together in Cartagena before they lost touch with each other. Vicente knew many of the writers present, and I was surprised to find he had read my novels as well.

"He's a literature freak," Leo said. "It's actually weird you guys never met."

"Do you write too?" I asked him.

"No, man, I'm a Bartleby. I'll leave that to you guys. Reading, that's my vice. Heavy metal and literature. Satan and Vila-Matas."

"Yeah, I got that sense. That you're a member of the cult."

"You guys are peas in a pod," Leo said. "I'll leave you to it."

I stood with Vicente at the corner of the bar and ordered two beers. We connected right away. And it really was odd that I'd never run into him at any of the literary evenings in Murcia.

"I don't get out of Molina much," he said when I asked. "Only for work. If I go out, I get drunk, and then I have to leave my car in Murcia. Parking and the taxi home cost me a small fortune. As does the whiskey, obviously."

We talked about literature for a few minutes. As Leo had noted, he was up to date on everything. He followed all the lit blogs and read all the big titles that year.

"Tell me, though," he said after asking what I'd been reading, "since we're supposed to be talking about your book, what is it exactly you need help with?"

I outlined what I was writing and could tell the story excited him.

"Jesus, that's hardcore. So this is like, the Murcian version of *In Cold Blood*?"

"Sort of." I smiled. "The thing is, I can't figure out how to access the court files, and I need them for documentation."

I told him I had tried a Civil Guard and had talked to a judge on the phone, but neither effort had gotten me anywhere.

"It's not easy," he said, "but you also have to know how to do things right. This isn't the first time I've come across a situation like this."

He grabbed his beer and took a long sip.

"There are journalists who've done it," he clarified. "Historians too."

"And it's legal?"

"Completely. Those archives are public. That's why they exist. And if the case in question isn't *sub judice*, then there's a thing called *legitimate interest*, and you can state that you have one, for whatever reason, really.

Plus, your interest sounds easy to justify. You're a writer, and you were a friend of the murderer, and a ton of years have passed. When did you say it was again?"

"1995."

"There's not going to be an issue, then. The hard thing, I'll go ahead and tell you, is actually finding the file. If it's from 1995, they'll have sent it to Zaragoza. It definitely exists, but getting the clerks there to move their ass and look for it . . . that's another matter."

"The name of the court and the investigating magistrate appeared in the news. I don't know if that helps."

"Not especially."

I showed him my phone.

"Oh, damn. Court number three. I was assigned there for a while. That's a different story. I might be able to pull some strings. It's your lucky day . . . Diego got the Setenil Prize, but you met me, that's not too bad either," he said, holding his beer.

No, it wasn't too bad. But it was unsettling. I write it now, and I realize that this series of coincidences lies at the edge of believability, far more than the flukes in a Paul Auster novel. Meeting Vicente, him working before in the same court that had overseen the crime, was almost a *deus ex machina*. But sometimes reality speaks to us in mysterious ways. And this novel had always been guided by the unexpected.

I thanked fate and treated Vicente to another beer. We exchanged numbers, and he promised he'd write or call when he knew something.

"You know you'll show up in the book, right?" I said.

"Change my name, I don't want to lose my job over literature. I might be Bartleby, but I'm not a dumbass. Not yet."

I got a text from him a few days later. *Murder case localized. File N° 9897/95. Mariví requested it from Zaragoza. She'll tell me when it's here. Two or three weeks, I was told. I'll write you and tell you how to fill in the petition for legitimate interest. The hard part's over. Ball's in your court, Capote.*

THE DRIVEWAY STARTS filling up with friends, who come with their parents. The parents go inside, the friends stay outside. Roberto's there, and Silvestre and Pedro Luis too.

The guys from the lowlands. At first, it was just Nicolás and you. Then they built the park, and the group started to grow. Not too big. Just five people, sometimes more. Roberto, who was in your class at Las Ramos, and Nicolás's cousins, Silvestre and Pedro Luis, who were two years younger than you. And Antolín, the son of the owner of El Yeguas, and the guys from your street and one or two from outside the village. Just enough people for a game. Five versus five. Three versus three. Two versus two, plus a goalie. In the park, in the fields in front of the chapel, or even in your driveway, with two stones for goals and chalk streak marking center field.

The guys from the lowlands. You went to the village fairs and you'd run out of energy after three games. You were the slowest. But you were good once you got the ball. Nicolás played midfield and never let anyone by.

He took it seriously, always. In championship games or when it was just the guys. He started off hard and never relaxed. Not even with you. You remember him kicking your ankles. The ball coming at you like a bullet when you played goalie. He was the one who kicked hardest. With rage. Clenching his teeth and nearly making the ball explode.

Where did that strength come from?

His fury. The same fury as when he beat everyone at arm wrestling. It didn't matter how strong his opponent was. He made everyone break. You could only stand him a few seconds. You've always been big, but you've never had an ounce of strength, and you've never known what fury was. Whereas his was in his eyes. The fury of the end. Because for him, everything was life or death. Soccer, tennis, dominos, cards, video games. He didn't want to lose. He didn't know how.

The same with chess. His final conquest. No one beat him at that either. Not even his cousin, Pedro Luis, the best strategist out of all of you. Sometimes the two of them would finish in a stalemate. Their games could last hours. No one ever took Nicolás's king, though. He was impervious. He protected what was his. The endless game.

You found them like that two days ago. On the wall where you're all sitting now. Nicolás and Pedro Luis, playing all evening, until Christmas Eve dinner.

That was the last time you saw him alive. You couldn't imagine what would happen a few hours later.

Nor does anyone imagine now—no one could—that Pedro Luis will be gone in a year too. Drowned in the sea, trying to fish out a ball that the waves wanted for themselves. You weren't there. But all the rest of those sitting on the wall with you crying were.

The guys from the lowlands . . . destroyed forever.

4

VICENTE'S MESSAGE CHEERED me up. Two or three weeks, he said. Either way, it was happening. Again, I felt like a character in a novel. I had an informer, he had requested a file for me, he would help me find the documents that were finally supposed to make sense of everything. Now I had to wait. The novel was in suspension. Reality had stopped. I had begun to think I'd have to push it forward by force. That need to keep the action going while the files were on their way was what led to my decision to visit the cliff.

I wanted to see the place where Nicolás had jumped. I'd known that since the project began. At some point, I'd even thought it might be a good way to finish the novel: me looking over the same ledge that Nicolás had thrown himself off of; me in the same place as the two people in the newspaper photo; me there, at last, twenty years later. That was where it had all ended. Where he leaped into the void. That could be the end of my novel, or at least one of its major scenes.

My brother Juan knew the way, and I called to ask him how to get there.

"I'll go with you if you like," he said after telling me the route.

"Don't worry, I'd rather go alone."

I wanted that moment to be intense: to find the place where Nicolás had jumped, climb El Cabezo and end the story, experience the sight of it in solitude.

"Don't get too close to the edge. The ground can open under your feet at any moment," he said before hanging up. I found that expression poetic, though I realized he must have meant it literally.

With the directions he gave me, I found the place on Google maps and chose my route. I chose to leave one Saturday morning after breakfast. And then it happened. I got into the car. I thought it over several times. I sensed that it wasn't right. But I wanted to do it. Go up to El Cabezo and see the place my friend had jumped from. But not from my own home. I would turn off for a few miles and start my journey from the driveway, replicating Nicolás's last drive. My body shivered from head to toe as I thought of it. I still didn't know why.

There are contemporary artists who also re-experience historical events, traveling and in this way bringing the past into the present. They call this historic recreation or reenactment. My own journey that day, too, would be a performance of history, I thought.

And if I left my GPS connected and allowed it to follow me, I would have an image on a map, a kind of drawing: the traces of foiled escape, the rubrics of death.

I meditated on this subject as I traveled the distance between my village and his driveway. It was lugubrious theatrics and I wasn't at all sure there was a point to it. I saw myself as an artist trying to make a drawing, remake a moment, recreate it. I toyed with the idea that writing was also this act of recreation, that I was going to revive the past, allow it to echo into the present.

I wondered what was the right path to take to El Cabezo. I remembered Antolín at El Yeguas saying he had seen him pass by that night, which meant Nicolás had gone up there the long way. Instead of cutting through Alquerías, he had crossed the solitary darkness of the lowlands. I wondered if, in his mind, he was looking for that woman who, according to his aunt, was trying to thumb a ride on the outskirts of the village. Or maybe it was just inertia. It didn't seem to matter for my trip, but as I drove, I kept thinking of it. For me, this was idle reflection, but Nicolás must have made his decision in a tenth of a second, anxious, images swimming in his head, terrified at what he'd just done. The car was his escape and his hideaway.

I saw all this: Nicolás scurrying from home, getting into his car, sliding in the key, trembling as he turned it, looking at his hands covered in blood, stepping on the clutch and speeding off, glancing at his own eyes in the mirror, or else avoiding them, conscious of what he'd done, eaten up by guilt and uncertainty, looking for a way out, for a way to make time stop.

I reached the driveway, turned around, hit start on my GPS, and crossed the lowlands toward El Cabezo with the strong sense that I wasn't alone. That some force was accompanying me. And in that moment, I was scared. At least, unlike Nicolás, I was making the journey during the day. I could have been more literary—more macabre—and left at three in the morning, or waited a month and a half longer to do it on Christmas Eve. But there was no need: Everything was traveling with me. I could feel it in my throat as soon as I began. Nicolás was there, the past was in that car, raising gooseflesh on my back and neck, all the way up my scalp.

I imagined the car as a Ouija board. That frightened me, and I sought a less forbidding image. A door through time. Nicolás and I had watched *Back to the Future* together. In his living room. Nicolás was one of the first people in the lowlands to have a VCR. I saw my Citroën C4 as a DeLorean traveling through time in a vortex where present and past touched. It wasn't crystal-clear, teleported immaculately between two eras as in movies. Instead, time itself was moving. Time and space entire. I could feel the car dragging everything along, leaving behind a wake, as though the atmosphere had thickened, the air grown compact. I could almost see it.

And that was why my car struggled forward, I thought. Nicolás's Seat 127 must have flown through those dark streets, but I was driving in slow-motion, staring at everything he had passed: the chapel, the substation, the long curve in the road, El Yeguas, the gypsy houses, the rest of it. . . . Then I reached the crossroads at the Reguerón River, and the present reasserted itself. The train tracks and the new highway had cut the lowlands in two, and that was where the replica of the past crumbled. Things weren't as I'd planned them: The old route was no longer there. But I kept going until I found the road that climbed El Cabezo. It hadn't changed much. It was better paved, with fewer potholes, but was just as treacherous, narrow and full of hairpin curves.

Again I felt Nicolás's presence. I imagined him barreling down that dark street. Looking in the mirror, I couldn't recognize my eyes. I tried to climb into his head. But I would never know what he'd thought. He was impenetrable. The guilt must have been terrible though. He had done the unimaginable... and for a few seconds, I could feel it. That same strange force that had gripped me in my dreams.

I drove through the village, passing Juan Alberto's house to the right. His old house—he had moved some time ago. Following my brother's recommendations, I continued for another mile until I found a crumbling home and a reservoir. That was the place.

I parked next to the roadside, feeling myself following in Nicolás's footsteps. Was this where he had parked too?

I got out, and found the tool shed I had seen on the news. There was a *for sale* sign posted there. The phone number, I assumed, belonged to one of his brothers.

The sun was shining bright, and it was warm for November. It felt more like spring than autumn. I walked slowly, looking for the cliff, getting tangled in the weeds, and imagined Nicolás running through blindly.

I couldn't stop thinking of the newspaper photograph. It reminded me of the protagonist of my previous novel, searching for the wall from the anonymous films he was writing about, trying to make his memories of this image coincide with reality. And I remembered myself a year and a half before, when I was in Ithaca and had traveled to the ruins of Folck's Mill to see the real wall that had inspired me to write the novel, this dragging fiction into reality.

I thought of all this as I looked for the cliff and felt in my flesh the *heterochronia* I had written about. Here, too, time held hands, past and present, image and veracity. When, in the United States, I had found the wall at Folck's Mill, I was moved to see the knotting together of fiction and reality superimposing themselves on each other. And I had thought that would happen here, this merging of time that would give meaning to my writing.

But when I crossed a rocky stretch and arrived there, fiction fell away, and what I was doing suddenly felt ridiculous.

Seeing myself there, like the wanderer above the sea of fog, made me question everything I'd done. It was a pointless simulacrum, and all at once, the action paused, the ropes holding the curtains broke, the lights came up, the backstage was revealed. Everything fell apart. The distance between the self that was there and the self I was pretending for dissolved. I could even feel the strain in my muscles.

What was I doing there? Who did I think I was? What the fuck was I playing at?

The sight of that abyss was like a sinkhole into which all my uncertainties drained. The performance had flopped and was now a parody. I was an imposter, with no idea what I was doing. I thought of that phrase of Marx's: first as a tragedy, then as a farce. The performance, the journey, my reconstruction of the past, was nothing more than that: a banal farce.

That was when I sensed that Nicolás was throwing himself into the void again, that I had brought him back from a pure desire to entertain myself by repeating the past, and in this way, I had killed him a second time. I could almost see his thin body running past me and flinging itself off. I didn't dare look down to see his shattered corpse on the floor of the ravine. I no longer cared about situating myself in the same place as the figures in the photo. I didn't want to imitate Juan Alberto's gesture as he pointed to where he'd found his cousin dead. The play was over. Literature had failed.

As I got in the car, I turned off my GPS. I had thought tracing out Nicolás's last steps would be poetic, clever, reinforcing the dramatic line running through the story. But now it struck me as ridiculous, obscene. I remembered what I'd scrawled out the day after my friend died. Neither letters, nor drawings, just the traces of gestures. Violent, filling an entire notebook that I later threw in the trash. Compared with them, the outline of my route on the GPS was an insignificant scribble.

I realized I hadn't photographed the place. I had found the real there, the nothing, the void. And that void had swept everything away. There was no possible representation. Images of it were pointless.

I returned home with the feeling that I was a fake. Nicolás was no longer with me. Reality had defeated literature. And my uncertainty about everything I'd written had grown. I began to question whether the story even mattered to me, whether I'd just been looking for an excuse to write a book.

My unease at having toyed with the past remained with me for days. If there were an ethics of writing, then I had crossed a line no sooner than I'd begun that journey. Or no: The journey had simply revealed what lay beneath everything this whole time, my turning the misfortunes of others into an object I could manipulate according to whim.

I went to my bedroom and looked through all I had written up to then. It was like a thriller: A writer returns to his past to write about a murder full of shadows. An investigation to find the hidden truth, the files that might reveal everything but never arrive.

It all sounded banal and insipid, just like the drive to El Cabezo. A performance. Toying with history.

The one sincere thing was my re-encounter with the past. The atmosphere in El Yeguas, the conversations with my brother, the walks through the lowlands, the memory of time forgotten. I began to sense that this was the real story I was writing about. My research into the murder had lit the wick, but the real crime I was writing about—the only crime I could examine myself—was the one I had committed with the past, with a self that was buried in time. As for what Nicolás had done, my conversations with the judge and Jiménez, my attempts to find an answer to all the open questions... who was I trying to deceive? All that was just obscene playacting.

It was then, I think, that I started to give up. I didn't want to go on pretending to be a detective or an artist of recollection. I wasn't even sure I wanted to go on pretending to be a writer. Not of this novel, anyway.

Everything felt heavy and opaque. The project had hit a wall. I could sense this. The pressure in my throat, the weight on my back, limited my movements in the days to follow. I needed to finish my *investigation*—how absurd that term sounded—as soon as possible. I didn't even care if I got hold of the court papers. I just didn't want to feel the nausea of imposture. The bitter aftertaste of the past vomited up once more. I had lost all relationship with the authenticity of events, with what it meant to write down the truth. Everything ended for me then and there, in the greatest of failures, in the grotesque conversion of history into cliché. Or so I thought for several weeks. Because then, coincidence—sorry, Paul Auster, but chance has its way in Murcia as well—intervened once more. That was when I found the photo. And with it, a bit of reality. The proof of a truth that I hadn't known how to hear before.

V

THE PAIN OF OTHERS

LOOK AT THEM there, it's like they're posing.

Someone says that as they enter the vigil.

All of them there. Sitting. On the wall. A compact composition. The guys from the lowlands.

Roberto unloads trucks at the paint factory. Silvestre helps his father with the tractor. Antolín slings beers behind the bar. Pedro Luis puts together windows in his brother's workshop.

You observe the picture, no longer there, and you feel the distance viscerally.

You have nothing in common with them anymore. A past, maybe, but not a present. Let alone a future. Or so you think. You've got new friends now. Your new friends read poetry, watch independent cinema, go to museums. They want to be historians, musicians, and artists. They live in a world the people from the lowlands know nothing about. They are where you've always wanted to be.

The city. The university. That was the ultimate distance. But you started moving away long before. When you did college prep and they took the vocational track. Even Nicolás. He could have studied if he'd wanted to. You never understood his decision not to. A mechanic, like his brother. You went to school at Beniaján; he went to Puente Tocinos. You hardly saw him after that. Your paths divided. Your presents, your futures. But there was still a past. And that held you together. All of you. The past that started to unravel.

Today, sitting on the wall, next to the guys from the lowlands, you know for sure that you are no longer in the frame.

You no longer live there.

It's long been a dead world for you.

1

AT THE END of November, I received an email from Javier Castro, an editor friend who had just published the diary of my time in Ithaca. He told me his girlfriend, Concha Martínez Barreto, an artist interested in the past and memory, was gathering an archive of photos of children in carriages. Such images had been commonplace since the beginnings of photography and were, he said, a repository for the dreams of childhood and the longing for paradise.

He asked whether I might have any such photos for her archive. I thought and responded that I did. In my childhood, I had briefly been obsessed with horses, and I clearly remembered there was a picture of me as a little boy in a small carriage being pulled by a pony.

I looked for it in the family photo albums, which I kept after my parents died. I was convinced it was there, and I turned the pages slowly, reacquainting myself with my childhood in the lowlands and glancing back at the photos of my first communion with Nicolás. I had seen them the summer before when I was trying to recall what he really looked like. His inexpressive face, his bangs over his eyebrows, his almond eyes were now so clear in my mind that the photos made little impression. After I had thought of him so much, his face was imprinted in my mind.

After fifteen minutes, I found what I was looking for. It wasn't in an album, but in a box of small photos I still needed to put in order one day. I looked at it for a few seconds. It was different from how I'd remembered it.

I was four or five years old, and wearing a red corduroy jumper and a green jacket. A gray pony was pulling my carriage. Next to me, the owner, Churrispas—a neighbor from the lowlands—was holding the reins in his hand. Standing next to the carriage in a blue shirt and checked canvas shoes, my father had his arm around my shoulders. The three of us were posing for the photographer, I assume my uncle Emilio. He always had his camera in his hands.

The carriage wasn't moving. Probably it never had. This was likely just a pose. But there was a carriage and a child. So it served the artist's purposes. I scanned it and sent it to Javier.

Perfect, he replied a few minutes later.

The scan of the photo remained a while on my computer screen. I had never seen it so big. It had always been tiny in memory, but now I could see it in detail. I blew it up and looked at the people in the background. My mother. My neighbor. My cousin Loles. All of them behind me, slightly unfocused.

And I was surprised to spy a slender person in the distance, visible to one side of Churrispas's knee. A girl, tall, dressed in black, her hair pulled back, her eyes lost. Alone, not taking part in the group.

I'd remembered that photo many times through the years, but I'd never seen her in it. I'd identified my mother's blurry face and the faces of my cousins, but I'd never looked close enough to notice her there. Only that afternoon did my eyes turn to her, as if she were calling to me. She had been there from the beginning, but only now could I see her, only now did I want to or know how: It was Rosi, in the very center, arms crossed, asserting her presence.

It's strange how the gaze can leave gaps. For years, Rosi had been an absence. Invisible in the photo, invisible in my memories, invisible, even, in my writing. My friend was the protagonist of my novel. She was a bit character, an empty silhouette that hardly even spoke in my dreams.

I remembered what I had told Murcian television about the two of them in an interview. I'd go there, I'd ask if Nicolás was there, and she'd go look for him. In my story, in my memory, she had been transparent, a blur in reality without presence, without a voice, without history.

In the newspapers, she was a nameless victim. Gender-based violence wasn't talked about then, and her tale didn't matter. It was the murderer who sucked up all the headlines. How could *he* have done that? She was the object of the action, but never its subject.

With her photo in front of me, finally noticing her face in the background, I realized I had fallen into the same trap. I had never given her the space she deserved. She used to call her brother to come play with me. She was still a no one. A name, an image, but not a story.

How could I repair this? Not easily, at this point. For weeks, I hadn't touched the novel. I'd been paralyzed since my drive to El Cabezo, lacking the strength to go on, and I'd thought I might give up on a frustrated project that had lost all relationship with the truth. But then that photo reappeared, and Rosi reclaimed her story. Her image spoke to me from the past, told me to go look for her, to ask myself what it was that had never been said or heard. That photograph felt like a sting inside. And I couldn't sidestep its demands. I had to open myself to her memory. Get to know her. So that she would never be a shadow again. So that I could look at that photo and always know that behind that figure, there had been a life. An existence torn up by the roots. A tale that could no longer be deferred.

THREE-THIRTY. THE FUNERAL starts at five, and it's your job to open the church. You feel it's all starting to end.

You go home and change clothes. You wash your genitals in the bidet. They stink of sperm and urine. You still haven't started showering every day. You don't even have your own cologne.

You open your father's bottle of Brummel and douse yourself in it. Then you get dressed. Gray polyester pants, black shirt, wool jacket, loafers. You look like a musty seminarian, and you smell like a tired old man.

You try to comb your hair, and you look at your face in the mirror. You can't know that it's in front of that mirror that they'll both collapse: first your father, then, later, your mother. You still don't know that this very place will be the center of what you will write: what's left in the mirror when you stop looking at yourself.

What's left in the mirror.

When you stop looking at yourself.

Over and over.

The mirror is still full of life for now. It reflects your boyish face, your bangs, your goatee without a mustache, your lost eyes, which for a moment seem to remain there on their own, bits of flesh stuck to the glass, dragged inward by a disembodied force.

You still don't know. This is vertical time, in front of you, condensed. Past, present, and future. Knotted in a single instant.

An invisible constellation.

2

"I CAN TELL you anything you want about her. Him I've wiped from my memory."

Those were the words of my cousin Loles when I called to ask if I could talk to her about Rosi. She had been her best friend, and when I started wondering who could tell me more about my friend's sister, I didn't hesitate to turn to her.

I hadn't talked to her in more than five years—almost since the death of her mother, Maruja. But when I told her that I was writing a book about what had happened twenty years ago, she was open and welcoming and invited me to come to her home whenever I wished.

"I think about her every day," she said before hanging up.

Loles was a few years older. We used to play together when we were little, but then one day, as a joke, she grabbed her brother's shotgun and aimed it at my head, not knowing it was loaded. I still have the scar between my eyebrows. It's one of my earliest childhood memories. A blurry one: my forehead bleeding, my brother Emilio, who didn't have his license yet, driving me to the hospital, the doctors trying to dig the birdshot out of my head. . . . My recollections are mingled with what others told me later. This remains a central moment of my past. Afterward, my relationship with my cousin changed. She was a girl when she shot me—no older than ten—she was just playing, and she had no way of knowing the gun was loaded. And yet, for a time, I couldn't help thinking she'd tried to kill me. When I grew up, I forgot all about it. My parents and brothers did too. The only one who held on to it was Nena. She couldn't turn the page, and until the end of her days always called Loles *the terrorist.* The people of the lowlands never forget. The past there is never fully past. I would find that out later, discovering that I was surrounded by stories from another time, rancor and family quarrels passed down from generation to generation that went back further than anyone could remember. Nena was the last of the people there for whom that event was as indelible as a stigma. We were different, fortunately: Time didn't affect us in the same way, and people didn't hold on to things forever. Or not in the same way. Me being shot became just another story and not much more. But I confess that when I dialed her number to talk to her about the past and about Rosi, a tiny part of me couldn't help but remember what had happened between the two of us in my childhood.

I waited for Christmas break, when I'd have a few days off, before showing up at her house one Friday afternoon. By chance—again, another coincidence, each stranger and less believable than the last—Loles had wound up living in one of the houses that shared a wall with Nicolás's: the home of Fina, the neighbor who used to knit under Julia's fig tree in the afternoons with my mother, Nicolás's mother, and my cousin's mother. The knitting circle, we called them.

Before ringing her doorbell, I stood staring at the gate that led to the yard. Like so many other people in the lowlands, they hardly used their front door, which opened into the living room. I had been in that yard more than once to retrieve the ball when we used to play soccer at Nicolás's place and someone kicked it over the wall. When I was young, the doors were always open. You'd walk in and announce your presence. There was no border between inside and out. Now, though, the gate was shut, just as the gate to Nicolás's home was shut. Those gates had long since ceased to be an unconditional invitation.

Loles opened the front door and guided me in. I felt relieved that I wouldn't have to go around to the back yard, following the same steps I used to take, just a few feet to the left, all those times on my way to Nicolás's room. Maybe that would have been more literary than walking straight into the living room, but it didn't matter, this was already a journey into the past. I had been there a few times in Fina's last months of life, when she was bedbound and my mother or Julia and I would visit her. The decor was different, but something from the old days persisted in that house, even with the toys on the ground, the plasma TV, the modern curtains, and the furniture from Ikea. The architecture of those homes recalls somehow another time in history, a time that never manages to be contemporary. The tiles, the walls, the structure itself, the air... it's as though they remain lodged in the past. I felt this as I sat on the sofa and my cousin made me a coffee. Time doesn't pass equally all over. Some places get stuck and can't move forward, lodged in the black holes of history that suck everything in.

"I sent Pepe and the kids out so we could be on our own," she said after filling up my coffee. Then she sat across from me in a chair of gray imitation leather, cracked in the corners, pulled the ceramic ash tray on the coffee table toward her, and looked straight at me. "So what do you want me to tell you about her? I wouldn't really know where to begin."

I didn't know where to begin either. So I told her the story I was writing and showed her the photo of the carriage. Seeing her, I said, made me realize I had no notion of who Rosi was, and that was why I'd decided to come.

Loles took the photo in her hands and looked at it for a few seconds.

"Ay, Rosi...," she sighed. "Always so fucking serious. But she was funny, you know... she'd make these random comments out of nowhere, and you'd just have to laugh."

She was pensive for a few seconds before lighting the first of ten cigarettes she would smoke one after the other, barely pausing, that afternoon.

"Do you mind if I record you?" I asked, opening the Notes app on my phone.

"Nah, go for it, keep a record of it for posterity."

It was the first time I'd decided to record a conversation. I didn't want to lose anything, and I wanted to be as faithful as possible to the truth. For some reason, I felt a responsibility to reality. And I wanted to attest to the life of a person I had never given a thought to before. An existence that, as I discovered that afternoon, had nothing special about it. Or rather, everything about it was special. Special in the way every normal life, every person's life, is special. Loles told me Rosi had been perfectly normal: not dull, not boring, just normal. Wonderfully normal.

Loles was a year older than Rosi, but they had been inseparable since they were girls. In the playground, in the afternoons, at Sunday school, at work.

"We were birds of a feather," she said.

Like Nicolás and me, I thought. And I remembered what María Ángeles had said—Miguel Ángel is Nicolás's skin—but I decided not to mention it just then.

Once she was old enough, Rosi quit school and started working at Tana, a fruit warehouse in the village. My mother had worked there too.

"Was she a bad student?" I asked.

"She was like me. Average. I quit school early and started working too. You didn't have to go to college back then. Now it seems like you're no one if you don't. And you look around and you see these kids who keep their nose in the books until their parents are in the poorhouse. Why am I telling you, you see it every day." I smiled. She was right. "Anyway, back then we were happy to just have some kind of job. We had a little pocket change, enough to go out and party. And Rosi was a saver, unlike the rest of us, who were a bunch of wild asses. Otherwise she was no different, though. Just a normal girl. She'd go out and dance like there was no tomorrow. She wouldn't get hammered like the rest of us, but if it was drinking time, she'd drink, no problem."

"Where'd you go out? El Cruce del Raal?"

"Yeah, almost always. Those were the good old days there. It got uglier later on."

I asked about El Cruce without even thinking. That was *the* place back in the nineties. At least for young people where we were from. The bars were all there, and the first dance club I ever heard of, called Snoopy. I never went, just as I never went to most of the dive bars on both sides of the road out there. Back then, I thought those places were like the devil's den. My parents had convinced me they were sinful. El Cruce del Raal was the worst. That was where young people went to drink and do drugs. The dregs of society. A whole generation going down the tubes. In summertime, you could occasionally hear the music from the door of my house. I remember my parents' conversations every time my cousin drove off: "Loles sure turned out to be a tramp. She goes out after midnight and doesn't come home till the sun's up. Shameless. One of these days she'll show up to Maruja's with a bun in the oven, and then the fun will be over." I'd hate to think what they'd say about me, their good, responsible little boy, if they saw me now.

"We used to go to the Radical too," my cousin said, "and sometimes to one of the hardcore clubs. Wherever the guys took us. Rosi was into it. She was a good girl, and she was serious, but she was also down for whatever."

I asked if she had a boyfriend back then, or if she'd ever had one.

"Yeah, same as everyone. She hooked up with guys. I mean, she was just a totally normal chick," she emphasized. "That last year, she really lost her head over this dude. But he kept blowing her off. The poor thing was actually in love with him. If she saw him out, she'd always say the night had been worth it, even if she didn't get to talk to him. And when we'd come back in the car blasting music, you could see a gleam in her eyes."

"What did you all listen to?"

"I don't know, just the stuff people listened to back then. A-ha. Tam Tam Go! Los Heroes de Silencio. Alaska, obviously, we listened to her all the time."

I told her Nicolás and I had never gone out partying, and I had never found out what kind of music he liked. Her expression changed in that instance.

"Listen, I'd rather not talk about him, OK? I know that piece of shit was your friend, but I can't even think about him without getting sick to my stomach. Even now. I was scared, you know? That could have been me."

"What?"

"That night. I could have easily run into him and I might have been the one he killed."

I hadn't planned on asking her about that night. I assumed it must have been hard for her. Harder than it was for me. And I just wanted to talk about Rosi and the happy times. But Loles went on: "We were supposed to go out that night. I was going to stop by her place at two. She was supposed to wait for me in the living room the way she usually did, she was going to come outside when she heard my car parking. That's how we always did. But that night, she stayed inside."

She snuffed out her cigarette in the ashtray and took another out of the metal case where she kept them perfectly lined up.

"I had been with some friends and I got tied up so I was twenty minutes late. I must have gotten there at two-twenty, I don't know, maybe a little after. Since she never came out, I just figured she'd gotten tired of waiting. But I got out of the car and rang the doorbell a couple of times just in case. No one answered, I pressed my ear to the door, I rang one more time, but I couldn't hear anything."

"The doorbell wasn't working?"

"It was disconnected. I found that out later. The Civil Guard didn't question me that night, but a week later an officer came to the pastry shop where I was working and we talked a little bit, I told him what I just told you and he said yeah, that Nicolás had disconnected the doorbell."

"That night?"

"Yeah, after he killed her. The officer said he was wearing socks when he did it and he tracked blood all over the house. There were footprints leading from her room to the front door. The bastard knew perfectly well what he was doing."

The image of Nicolás in blood-soaked socks walking over the light-colored tiles took shape in my head, almost palpable: the white cotton of his socks stained red. The marks of his feet.

"He had just killed her. The fucker. Literally right then. His parents said they had gone to bed at one-thirty. And by two-twenty, the doorbell was already disconnected."

"What about the car?" I asked. "Was it still there?"

"Yeah. He was still at home. He might even have seen me at the door. If I'd gotten there on time, maybe he wouldn't have killed her. Or maybe he would have killed me too."

As she said this, her eyes filled with tears, and she fell silent. She got up and walked to the other room. A few seconds later, she returned with a fresh supply of cigarettes, which she slipped slowly and carefully into their case.

"My Pepe spends the whole afternoon rolling these, and then I smoke them all in one sitting," she said, drying her tears with the back of her hand.

Then she lit one and continued, "I got back home at five, and that's when I saw the whole spectacle: the Civil Guard's cars, people standing at the gate. And you know the worst part...?"

"What?"

"I was afraid it might happen. I knew something bad was coming. You'll probably think this is stupid, but there was like an eclipse those days, and when I was driving to El Cruce that night, I got a bad feeling. The whole night I felt out of sorts. I told your sister-in-law's sister, she used to go out with us, I was like, *It's weird that Rosi didn't come out tonight, right?* And she told me she must be tired. I said, *Yeah, sure*, but something about it didn't sit right with me."

I looked at her, trying to understand.

"And then," she added, "well, you can imagine. It was just terrible. For two years, I could hardly raise my head. Those were the worst years of my life. I was taking drugs all the time. I couldn't be alone. I couldn't sleep. I kept thinking he'd come back for me. I nearly lost my mind. Your sister-in-law's sister was the same way. We started to imagine that Rosi was with us every time we'd go out. That she was in the back seat pushing us. I know you'll think I'm crazy, but we could feel her. Literally every time we got in the car. We never said anything, but then one night we looked at each other at the same time. It felt like someone was kicking the back of the seat. Call it the power of suggestion or whatever, but we sensed it, both of us, at the same time. We didn't want to talk about it, anyway, we weren't scared. It was him we were scared of. Not her. I loved her like a sister. She wasn't going to hurt me, right? Like I told you, I couldn't say a bad word about her. All my memories of her are good, right up to that fucking Christmas Eve. Since we were little, we spent some of the best moments of our lives together. Playing Chinese jump rope in Julia's doorway while she knitted under the fig tree. If only I could be that innocent again..."

I stayed sitting there on the sofa, empty coffee cup in my hand, absorbed in a conversation that had begun as an interview and had turned slowly into a monologue. More than a writer, more than a detective, I felt like a psychoanalyst, a confessor, a listener for someone who needed to be heard.

"What a coincidence, right?" she said. "I end up moving here, right next door to her old house. Rosario liked that, I think. I guess I reminded her of her daughter. When she'd go grocery shopping, she'd buy bags of snacks and toss them over the wall to my kids. The poor old woman, she died of grief."

"I'm not surprised."

"You know what she said to Asunción before she died? That she couldn't believe that I was her daughter's best friend and didn't go to the wake or the funeral."

"You must have been a wreck," I responded.

"That too. But I couldn't go in that house and stand there in front of the coffin of that bastard who killed my friend. I would have spit on it."

"Sure..."

"When they took the coffins to the church, I tried to look, but even then, I couldn't take it. I just couldn't. I can't bring myself to remember him or even think about him. I've erased him from my memory."

As she spoke, I thought about how different everything was from her perspective. Loles had no contradictory feelings about Nicolás. He was a killer, and that was it. There was no more to it. He deserved to be dead.

"There are people who say his brothers went up there and threw him off," she added.

"Garre told me that," I told her. "I don't believe it, though."

"Sure, yeah. Me neither. But if he'd been my brother, that's what I'd have done, I can tell you that. Push him off, kill him. With my own two hands."

I don't know how I reacted, but she froze for a minute before continuing: "Look, I know he was your friend, and I'm sorry to talk this way, but . . . I mean, why do you think he did it? Have you ever asked yourself that? You must have some theory. Why would he fucking go crazy and kill his sister like that?"

I wasn't sure what to say at first. I didn't feel like sharing what I began to consider the afternoon I spoke with the judge. "I . . . ," I began. "All I know is him killing himself is probably the best thing that could have happened. Because otherwise, he'd be out on the street. And that would be hard to take."

"I couldn't have dealt with it. I'd have had to move somewhere else. The idea of seeing him around here . . . knowing what he did. I don't even want to think about it. No. I'd rather hold on to the good memories. How we used to laugh. How we used to joke around. Our teenage years were incredible. Those were the happiest time of my life."

She paused and lit the last cigarette of the evening.

"Sometimes I think about what her life would have been like. If she'd have gotten married or what job she might have. I mean, I'm almost fifty, and here I am, unemployed with three kids. I can't say if I'm happy. Sometimes I think I am. But I'm not always convinced. And I have this thought that I left a part of myself behind, that it died with her. Or, I don't know, maybe it's the other way around, like I could never fully mature because I'm stuck in that night and I can't figure out how to escape it. I'm not a philosopher like you, and I don't know how to put what I'm feeling into words. But sometimes these things pass through my mind. If I knew how to write them, I would."

We went on talking the rest of the evening, moving back and forth from her memories of Rosi to her life today. Her husband, her kids, her struggles to make it to the end of the month. I felt at ease sitting with her. As if we were finally having a conversation that had been a long time coming. I even forgot to look at my phone, and when I finally did, I saw an alert that said I'd run out of memory. I didn't know how much I'd managed to record. But it didn't matter. That conversation had sunk in deep. The concrete details were barely significant. Even the references to the night when it had all happened. What had mattered that night was that I'd put myself in another's place. For the first time in my life.

As my cousin spoke, I had the feeling that Rosi was coming back to life, that she could breathe again. Not in the macabre way that she and Nicolás haunted my dreams, but authentically, and I knew: There had been more life in that conversation than in anything I had written thus far. Despite the sorrow and the pain evoked, Rosi had come back to life for a moment. And for the first time, I had felt sincere compassion. Rosi had been a story, a body full of feelings, a life. And Nicolás had been the shadow that had taken it all away.

When we were done talking, it was eight at night, and the sunlight had long since ceased to brighten the windows. We walked outside, and Loles followed me to where I'd parked. Before I took off, I thanked her for everything she'd said.

"Thank you for listening. It was nice to remember her."

"It was nice for me to get to know her," I responded.

"We'll see what comes out of all this."

"Something good, I hope."

"There's only one thing people need to know," she concluded. "That she lived, that she was happy, and that he killed her. There's nothing else to say. See how quick I wrote your book for you?"

ON THE ROAD, you find Odin, Nicolás's cat. He too seems disoriented.

He's a Siamese, like your cat, Lira. They shared the same mother. They were the two that survived from that litter.

You can't forget the scene. The cat giving birth, and Nena drowning the kittens in a bucket. One after the other.

Your cousin Carlos is even crueler. Just once, you saw him do it. That was all you could take. He puts the cats into a plastic bag and smacks it against the wall. The crunching of the tiny bones turns your stomach.

You have crucified frogs, burned ants with a magnifying glass, blown smoke into bats until they explode. Because you wanted to be like the older kids. Like your cousin Carlos. And so you tried to smile while he bludgeoned the cats or shot out their eyes. That was the lowlands. That was childhood. That was childhood in the lowlands.

Nicolás never did anything like that. He always got scared. The afternoon he saw your cousin beating the cats against the wall, he ran off, and he didn't come back up the road for several days. Maybe that's why you convinced your mother to let the cat keep two of her kittens next time. One of them is Odin. Maybe he recognizes you, and that's why he meows and winds his body around your legs. He's looking for his owner. He doesn't know the violence and savagery finally caught up to him.

3

WHEN I GOT home, I had a quick dinner and sat down to transcribe the conversation. I didn't even open my Notes app. I had everything in my head. As I wrote in my notebook, I began to feel I could finally bring my stalled novel to an end. Putting down what I'd learned about Rosi reconciled me with all I had used and rendered tawdry about the past. I hadn't learned much that I hadn't known. But I knew something now. And that opened the possibility of another story, another point of departure. Rosi was no longer a blurry silhouette. At least, not for me. And yes, this was probably where I should bring the book to a close. With the echo of a normal story, a life ended from one day to the next, shorn off by my best friend.

Rosi's story made me keep believing in the meaning of this book. I had managed to pull from the darkness, at least for a few seconds, an image that had been a mere background to my memories. A minimal movement. A glimpse of reality. A glimmer of justice. A part of the other side, of the pain of others.

What happened afterward didn't matter that much. When I got a WhatsApp message from Vicente after a few weeks, everything was already drawing to a close. And what for many would have been the culmination of the story was for me a coda, an afterthought. What mattered had already taken place.

Capote, his message read, *the file's at the courthouse. Mariví called and told me. I'll write you in detail to tell you how to fill out the form you'll have to turn in to the court clerk. They'll be there Monday or Tuesday morning.*

An email arrived that afternoon with instructions on how to complete the petition of legitimate interest. It was several pages long, with all the articles I was supposed to refer to and how to best phrase my motivation for researching the case. Vicente had taken this to heart, calling, giving me advice, pulling strings... he had done more than even a close friend would. There are people who go through the world trying to avoid others, as if they were an obstacle; and there are others—and Vicente was a clear example—who will give their all to help a complete stranger. Though his email arrived just as it was dawning on me that my work was really behind me, when I saw all he'd done, I knew it wasn't enough just to send a message, and I called to thank him.

"For once, I can make a contribution to literature," he joked.

"Seriously, I can't tell you how grateful I am that you went to so much trouble."

"Fuck it, just write a good book, OK? That's what you've got to do."

"I'm working on it."

"Yeah, so like I said, take the form down there on Monday or Tuesday. They've changed the official title, now it's Justice Administration Specialist, but whatever, it's still a court clerk you need to talk to, same as always. By the way, eat your breakfast before you head over. I don't know if you'll be in the mood after. Apparently everything's in there, crime scene photos, the autopsy, all of it."

VI

THE SHADOW ZONE

IT TAKES YOU five minutes to reach the chapel and open up with your mother's keys. You play the organ here, you read the scripture, you toll the bells. You used to come here with Nicolás. Now you have to come alone. This is where you'll say bye to him.

Today, every corner reminds you of him. Everything is a snapshot of the past.

The sacristy: the two of you waiting for the priest to arrive, measuring the distance from one wall to the other, inventing games only you know the rules to.

The altar: the two of you stationary, flanking the priest, taking bets on who will move first. Then kneeling during the blessing of the sacramentals, or ringing the bell, two seconds longer than expected, or one second less. Or waiting there as long as you can. *This is the sacrament of our faith. We announce your death, we proclaim your resurrection, Lord Jesus Christ.* The two of you behind the altar, hidden until the last second, holding your breath, as if you were underwater.

The offerings: one with the collection plate, one helping the priest clean the chalice and prepare for communion, trying to act as one, keeping time, running when the church is full or slowing down when hardly anyone is there.

You don't know if you believe in anything. You've never known. But the church is a playground. A happy memory.

Now, as you prepare it for the funeral, you sense that this happiness is gone forever.

1

IN MOVIES AND novels, it all happens in the blink of an eye. A guy takes an interest in a crime, and boom, he's got the files in hand with all the information he needs. I needed a year and a half to get those papers, and my heroism was scant, basically nonexistent. There wasn't much literature to it, and I thought of how ridiculous the whole thing had been. At the same time, though, it had been hard.

I had taken my time in part because I was never certain I wanted to see those papers. That uncertainty had motivated the novel. The question of whether I was prepared to face the naked truth. At some point in my research, I told myself I did, that I wanted to know, but slowly, I became convinced that I'd deceived myself. And in a way, the truth I was looking for when I started I had already found through other avenues. It was a minor truth, one built of minimal certainties. But the truth of what had happened that night, the truth I could find in the report, the truth that would answer all my questions... it no longer interested me.

And yet, I kept going. I did it to avoid disappointing Vicente, who had shown so much interest in the matter, and for all the people who had followed the evolution of my writing. I felt obliged to press on, as if I now had some sort of commitment to them—to a *them* that was abstract and immaterial. But I confess that morbid curiosity also got the better of me. Those papers were the object of a long unsatisfied desire. And now I would have the satisfaction of seeing, of knowing. Maybe that, more than anything else, is what made me get up early on the first Monday of February 2017 and show up at the Palace of Justice with a form alleging legitimate interest to look into the file of Rosi's murder.

That morning, court number three was bustling, several employees had been sent to another part of the building, and it was difficult for me to find the person I needed. I got lost in the labyrinth of hallways and couldn't help but notice the contrast between the elegant lawyers with their immaculately combed hair, their briefcases and shiny shoes, and the accused and the little people in tracksuits with bags under their eyes and stubbly beards.

It all reminded me of *The Middle Ages*, a novel by my friend Leo, an X-ray portrait of the world of the court. I'd found it seductive when reading, but I could never have imagined how true-to-life his portrait of the passivity of civil servants was. Not, at least, until that morning, which dragged on until it dawned on me that I wasn't likely to see the files that day.

I had waited nearly an hour for the person at the counter, had left my number so they would call me when the clerk returned, had gone out for a coffee and come back an hour later and gotten lost again in the hallway when finally, the clerk deigned to see me.

They're gods, you're mortal, I recalled Leo once telling me.

I removed my cap for formality's sake and tried to act cordial and unassuming.

The clerk received me in a small office filled with file boxes. The blinds were drawn, and hardly any light was filtering in, and that made everything far grimmer than it might have been otherwise. The man, with greasy yellowish hair and a dark gray V-neck sweater, reminded me of an aged high school teacher. Indeed, his nasal voice, his way of speaking to me without looking me in the eyes, evoked for me my own teacher, Mr. Adolfo, who even when I had known him seemed like a relic of an earlier time.

"Let's hear it," he said after shaking my hand with all the effusiveness of an automaton.

"I've got a legitimate interest petition here to see some court documents. If I'm not mistaken, you've already been informed."

He took the paper and examined it deliberately, with the attitude of a person bothered when he has far more important tasks at hand.

"It says here you're a . . . writer."

I nodded.

The word *writer*, coming from him, sounded very different from when Vicente had said it. There was a note of scorn there that reminded me of how Garre down in the lowlands had referred to me as an *intellectual*.

"And that you were a friend of the murderer, and you were interviewed on the day of the crime."

"That's correct."

"Do you have that interview?"

"Yes," I responded, not really knowing what he was getting at. "I can show you the video of it on my phone."

"Do that."

As I scrolled through my photos and videos, the clerk, who never told me his name, continued examining the petition, as though trying to make a decision. The mood was tense. I wanted to be nice, but it was hard with his brusque questions and reactions.

"Here it is," I said. "I had hair back then, but it's me."

He took my phone and watched the video. This was the one time I detected a hint of a smile on his face.

"Well," he said, dragging over a faded folder on one corner of his desk, "everything you were looking for is here."

I hadn't realized the folder had been in front of me the whole time. In fact, it was the only thing on the table. The clerk had apparently been waiting for me all morning, though his attitude indicated anything but that.

He opened the grubby folder, which had several documents held together by staples, and looked through it as I stood there across from him watching. "You've got here," he said, "the Civil Guard's investigation, the declarations, the autopsy report. There are photos too, but...you can't see those."

"Excuse me?"

"The photos can't provide you with any new information about what took place."

For a moment, I didn't know how to react. Then I managed to say, "Look, in my novel, the images are as important as the facts."

"Fine," he responded, as though he hadn't paid attention to what I'd said. "But you can't see them. They're not relevant to your research, and . . . moreover, there's sensitive material."

He kept looking impassively at the documents as he said this, eyes lost in the photos. "No . . . ," he went on, "you can't see these." And he continued flipping through them as if they were a home décor magazine.

The photos there amid the dog-eared papers had a grim glow. I could make out a few things from where I stood: the floor of the bedroom covered in blood, a pair of feet, a white nightgown, footprints . . . not much more.

He looked at them coldly. I sensed them and trembled. What little I could see, what I could imagine, still remains frozen in my mind.

The clerk realized I was staring into the folder and slammed it shut. After a moment's hesitation, he concluded, "No, you can't see them. They're not relevant for what you're trying to find out. I can't allow you to access them."

"Fine," I said, since we were going around in circles. "If it can't be done, it can't be done."

He relaxed when he saw I wouldn't press him. "The rest of the file we can photocopy for your consultation.

You'll just have to tell me what it is you think is relevant." *Relevant.* That word ricocheted in my mind. As if I could convey what was relevant. He continued, "We can then photocopy it for you."

"Honestly, I'd take everything," I said.

"The reconstruction of the crime scene?"

"Yes."

"The sketch of the room and how the bodies were found?'

"Yes."

"The parents' statement?"

"Yes."

"The brothers' statement?"

"Yes."

"One of them says here the murderer almost never spoke. Strange, no?" He went on paging through, and asked, "Forensic analysis?"

"Yes."

"For the victim and the murderer?"

"Yes," I repeated, "everything but the photos."

He made sure my phone number and email address were on the form and told me they would be in touch when the copies were done.

Before saying goodbye, he turned the pages of the file once more. I don't suppose his intentions were bad, but it struck me as a way of showing that he could see all that I wasn't allowed to. He was the owner of this sensitive material, and I had to throw myself at his feet to consult it.

“The clerk you got was a little . . . special,” Vicente remarked later when I called him to tell him how my appointment had gone. “I guess you didn’t notice his last name. If you had, you’d have realized you’re no one to him.”

THE HOUR IS nigh. The tolling for the dead. You clutch the rope of the bell at the top of the tower and pull out the slack before you ring it. You do the same for the bells lower down. You've been doing this since you were a child. You used to have to jump off the ground and dangle from it. You used to need Nicolás to help you. Now your arms alone are enough, and you can hold it until the clapper strikes.

Slowly, the people gather at the door. Conversations, whispers, murmurs. The final toll provokes silence.

The hearses arrive, and everything happens in slow motion. You can see it from the belfry.

They take out the coffins and local men bear them on their shoulders. One, then the other. You don't know which casket holds your friend's body.

The priest is waiting on the threshold, praying before they're taken inside.

Not a single person more can fit. The chapel is small, and there are people everywhere. You manage to wedge yourself into a corner.

You won't be an altar boy today. Nor will you play

the organ. Not even a funeral march. Father Pedro has decided silence is best.

But you will have to read. Read, the way Nicolás did so many times.

When the priest sits and you climb the pulpit, you feel everyone's eyes on you. And you hear the murmurs.

That was his friend, someone says.

When you pass the coffins, you can't avoid touching them. The memory of the cold wood on the back of your hand will never leave you.

You clear your throat and you read without raising your eyes from the book.

Reading from the Book of Lamentations: *And I said, My strength and my hope is perished from the Lord: Remembering mine affliction and my misery, the wormwood and the gall. My soul hath them still in remembrance, and is humbled in me. This I recall to my mind, therefore have I hope…*

You are reading for yourself, and you're reading for Nicolás. His voice and yours, at once. That was how you read the gospels during Holy Week. The passion and the death of the Lord. The two of you together: *When Jesus therefore had received the vinegar, he said, It is finished: and he bowed his head, and gave up the ghost.*

You were the voice of the narrator. He read the dialogues. The priest was Christ. Sometimes, Nicolás was Christ too. But you were always the narrator.

Every year, you read it better. The neighbors used to

say so on their way out of Mass: That's the best part of the service, hearing the word of God.

Now your voice is trembling. Your eyes are filled with tears. You can hardly see the last words of the psalm.

And he shall redeem Israel from all his iniquities.

You are almost inaudible. Yet everyone responds:

I wait for the LORD, my soul doth wait, And in his word do I hope.

2

THE COURT CLERK'S decision put an end to all possibility of a raw confrontation with the photos. Despite my disappointment, I was relieved. I've written essays about the representation of violence, I've seen extreme films and performances and harrowing, even repulsive images; I'm supposedly immune to fright, but I'm not sure I could have handled the sight of something so close to my own experience.

When I was planning the book, I had imagined that moment many times. And I'd come to the conclusion that, when I finally saw those pictures, I wouldn't try to describe them. I would let them bore into my eyes, I would narrate my reaction, but I wouldn't reveal their contents to the reader. I would bear the weight of them myself, but I would keep them away from the eyes of the spectator, as the Chilean artist Alfredo Jaar had done with *The Eyes of Gutete Emerita*, showing not the cadavers mutilated in Rwandan genocide, not the bodies without names and without stories, but the gaze of one who has seen death up close.

I was certain I would never copy those photos of Rosi and Nicolás or snap pictures of them with my phone.

Those images were not to be reproduced. I had even hoped that seeing them would banish them from my mind: that I would see to erase, fixing the details of that which had been vague all the better to forget it. Or at least I would try.

But now, none of what I had imagined would happen. Those photos would remain out of sight. Not because I wanted to leave them out, but because I couldn't view them. And this was liberating. I began to think that the apathetic gentleman had been right, and that they really hadn't been *relevant*—I grinned as I used that word he kept uttering at the courthouse. What would seeing them solve? At most, they would have re-victimized the victim. Seeing Rosi in her nightgown, covered in blood, would be like killing her again. Contemplating Nicolás's body, shattered after the fall, would bring me

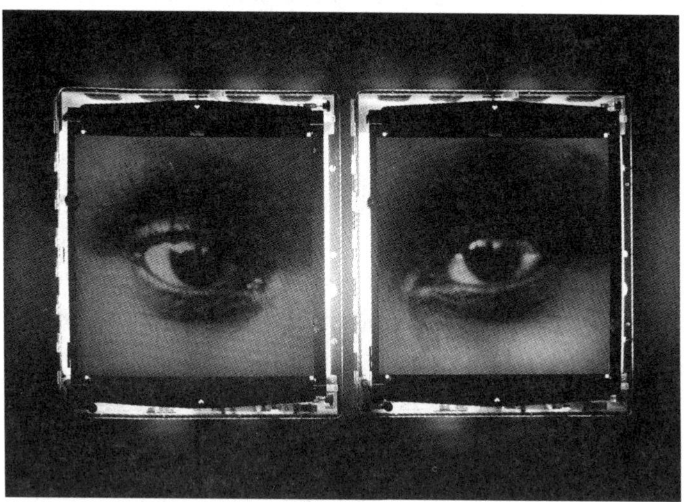

no closer to the truth. In the era of transparency, when everything must be seen, said, and known, perhaps certain images must remain forever on the other side of the mirror, beyond vision, the inverse of the gaze.

The photos would have shown everything. More than a thousand words. But the thousand words were what I could still expect. Or so I thought for a few weeks. I imagined the files would contain some revelation. And I had the sense I'd done my writing and research out of order. I had been documenting myself for all those months, whereas now was when I ought to have begun writing. Now, when I had gathered everything, when I had spoken to witnesses, seen the TV footage and the newspaper clippings, was about to receive the court documents, when I had all the evidence and all the facts that could be proven. Starting with the truth, with reality. For a moment, that's what I believed. But that would have been a different novel. Not the novel I wanted to write. Among other things because, once everything was laid out, I didn't want to write anymore. What I'd thought and written was what had brought me to this point. A point that for many would have been the beginning, but for me was the end, the coda to a story I had deemed finished some time ago.

I thought all this as I awaited news from court number three, checking my email every morning and looking at my missed calls. Of course, I was expecting something. The search would be over soon, regardless of what I found. But a part of me couldn't relax, prey to a forbidding sensation similar to what I'd felt when I'd stood in front of the cliff Nicolás had jumped from. What if examining those pages drew me back toward imposture?

I felt once more that pressure in my throat and back. And my unease grew as the weeks passed. One day I woke and couldn't see out of my left eye, and it took almost a month to recover my vision. A stye that had hardened into a cyst. A symptom of stress, the ophthalmologist told me. I chalked it up to work, travel, emotional difficulties that were a novel in themselves, a novel I might even write one day. But at bottom, as I realize now, I didn't want to keep going. I couldn't. I had carried this story around inside me for too long and I needed it all to end. Now. My body was expelling it, manifesting its unwillingness to keep holding it inside. And so, when one morning in April I received an email from the court clerk with the decision on my request, instead of turning indignant, I felt I could finally breathe again.

Under the heading *Resolution of Request for Information*, I read:

> In conformity with Article 7 of Royal Decree 937/2003 of July 18 on the modernization of judicial archives, which states that "documents that may **affect the safety of persons, their honor, their privacy, their family, and their reputation** may

> not be consulted by the public without the express consent of those affected unless **a period of 25 years has passed after the incident in question** if the date is known, or 50 years from the date of the documents themselves," and in view of the clear relation between the information contained in the court files and possible harms to the privacy and reputation of the concerned parties, access to the **requested documents** is DENIED, as the period limiting public consultation has yet to expire.

For several minutes, I didn't know what to do. I was at home, putting the finishing touches on the text for an exhibition catalogue, and I lost all my concentration. Unable to think clearly, I called Vicente and told him what had happened.

"That fucking clerk got scared," he exclaimed. "He decided to stick to the letter of the law. You should appeal. Send me the resolution. You've got a legitimate interest. There's got to be a way for you to get access."

I sent him the email and walked outside to clear my head. I stopped at the hill bordering the Segura River and sat a few minutes on a bench that looked straight into the lowlands. The blue of the April sky struck me as more intense than usual. I took off my cap and felt the warm sunlight directly on my scalp. Everything had become suddenly more real, more tangible, including my ideas, which were ordering themselves slowly in my mind.

Twenty years ago, my best friend killed his sister and threw himself off a cliff. That was how the novel would begin. Twenty years, the time needed to write. But now there was another time frame: twenty-five years for the pain to stop hurting. A random quantity. Why should twenty years hurt and twenty-five not? Why should the reputation of those affected be safe after twenty-five years? Why would the past then cease to be present? Are wounds supposed to heal from one year to the next?

I meditated on these arbitrary designations and the contingencies of my own writing. If I'd started this project a few years later, the ending would be utterly different. The ending, and probably the entire story.

At any rate, time was no excuse. Twenty-five years seemed like a lot, but the truth is, there were only three left and they'd soon be over. I could let everything lie and devote myself to other things. It wasn't as if I made my living writing. Yes, I could wait, but it wasn't about timing or deadlines. The law actually helped me finish, it freed me from a burden I could no longer bear. Despite deceiving myself with the notion that I wanted to learn the truth—the truth I had hoped to find in the files—in my heart, I didn't need to know. Or at least, I didn't need to know *that*. Because I would never find the why or the answer to my questions. All I could hope for were facts, information, the exact hour of the murder, the instrument Nicolás used to kill her, how many times he struck her, what route he took to El Cabezo, how long he had waited before jumping, the color of the belt he'd slung around his neck.... Forensic precision. Investigative transparency. That would be there in the stapled sheets of the file. Things which, in the words of the law, *could cause possible harms to the privacy and reputation of the concerned parties.* Things that happened to be precisely what I wasn't interested in finding out.

Then there was the other question. That I won't deny. The need to know if Nicolás had tried to rape Rosi. That may have been the one doubt that still beset me. But more and more, I thought I knew. Everything hinted that he had. The maxi pad on the ground, my cousin's remarks, the neighbors' words, the judge's hints, what Abellán had confessed... maybe they were just rumors, but they stuck with me. And a part of me had given up on knowing. It was possible that Nicolás had raped Rosi. I will write that again now. It's even possible that there was something between them, and it wasn't the first time he did it or tried to. I'll never know. And the court files probably can't clarify that either. There may only be hypotheses, theories, speculation. With a basis in fact, perhaps, but speculation nonetheless.

And did I really need to know? Was this *legitimate interest* or morbid curiosity? What right, I asked myself, do we have to know the lives of others? I wasn't a policeman, I wasn't a detective, I wasn't even a journalist. I was just a writer—or an art historian who thought of himself as a writer—one who was playing at digging into the past. Why had I allowed myself to look into the keyhole, to make myself a privileged spectator to the tragedy? What special privileges did I have over others?

Sometimes, we write to learn. Other times, we write to know when to stop. And then there are times when we write to learn to accept that there are things we can't always know.

Sitting on that bench by the river, in a silence softly broken by the cars driving through the city, I began to think that, unlike what had happened as I was writing this book, what was happening now was more like life than a novel. It had the structure of reality, not of fiction. A structure that breaks off in a moment when so much has yet to come out, that abandons us without letting us learn all that we'd hoped to learn, that doesn't resolve what it had intended to resolve; a perpetual dissatisfaction that literature exists to cure, putting an end to the search, revealing the cause, granting us the object of our desires so we may rest easy, satisfied with the illusion of plenitude and completion that gives us peace of mind.

None of that was going to happen here. Those papers, whatever they contained, would remain out of sight, like the images that accompanied them. First, because the law demanded it, but also because I wasn't prepared to look at them. Despite having been so close, despite touching them with my fingertips. Despite the notion that inside them lay the key to everything. The time for them was over. Their truth didn't belong to me. And if there was some key in them, still, my pursuit of it had guided me into the present, an awareness that sometimes you get tired of wanting to know, the conviction that writing—and living, if we're honest—is sometimes tantamount to renunciation.

"I made it this far," I said aloud, I think, as I stood up off the bench to go home.

And as I did so, my body felt light, as if those words had lifted a weight from me. And I felt a strange airiness on my way home. Especially when, before going upstairs, I phoned Vicente and said, "We're not going to appeal."

"What?"

"I've been thinking it over. It's better this way."

"Are you sure? Our chances aren't great, but they're not nothing. You really ought to try."

"I appreciate everything you've done for me, but no. I mean it this time. *I would prefer not to.*"

YOU CAN GO in peace. The sun hasn't fallen yet, but it won't take long.

As the coffins emerge from the chapel and return to the hearses, you toll the bells again, and the silence returns. Even now, you don't know which coffin belongs to Nicolás. Maybe the men carrying them on their shoulders don't know either. Maybe only those who won't stop crying do.

Before it's all over, a line forms, and the people give their condolences: the neighbors, your parents, Julia, your brothers, your cousins, and even your friends, the guys from the lowlands. Everyone but you, who watch the scene from afar.

What will you say? I'm sorry? What would be the point?

At a certain moment, their mother looks at you. Rosario. Her expression isn't like their father's. It's not a nothingness, not an abyss. It is desolation, defeat, infinite pain. But not emptiness. Rosario looks at you, and in her ravaged face, you see something resembling affection. You don't need to come over, Miguel, I know what you're feeling, I know you're hurting too. That's what she seems to be saying. Her eyes and yours harbor the same pain. You feel her agony. And you can sense that she feels yours too.

Compassion. Feeling with another. Feeling the distance. The distance you watch from as the scene draws to an end.

The cars leave, the people disperse, the chapel empties out. It's over. At least what you can see, what happens in front of your eyes. Because offscreen, there's still much more to go. In the cemetery, a place you've never been, not even to visit your grandfather's tomb. You don't yet know how many times you'll go there and watch coffins slide into the mausoleums. How many times you'll see the worker build a tiny wall of bricks over the crypt and smooth it over with mortar. How many times you'll pray an Our Father and mourn those you've loved.

You still don't know anything. Not even that you will soon hear the crackling of time, the crunching of memory, the murmur of the dark wound that will cloud your memories.

You are eighteen, and the future hasn't begun.

You are eighteen, and all you know is that it hurts.

3

I DIDN'T THINK much about it, nor did I force myself to make it too literary. I wanted this time, by any means, to avoid the sensation of imposture. Now, as I write, it's becoming a scene, but at the time, I tried—I swear I did—to escape the character, the novel, and all the narrative structure I had created around the story.

It was a Tuesday morning after class. I didn't want to wait anymore. There was no need to. I bought flowers on the way, at the first florist I came across. I walked through the cemetery with the bouquet of pink and white carnations in my arms and left it at the foot of the mausoleum where Rosi and Nicolás lay. Where their mother, Rosario, lay too.

The cemetery was almost deserted, and from the mausoleum, I could just hear the conversation of the workers who had greeted me on entering. The sun was shining with peculiar intensity, as it had in the preceding days. Its light blinded me a few seconds, and I struggled to make out their name plates behind the glass that protected them. When my eyes adjusted, I was surprised to find three small red lamps burning in a corner of the tomb and a handful of white carnations in each of the tiny metal vases hanging from the marble plates. Someone had visited recently. Instinctively, I turned: Maybe they were still there. But no. There was no one. I was alone. Completely alone.

Turning back to their crypts, I stared at Rosi's photograph. Her face wasn't strange to me. I recognized her features. I could imagine her alive. Everything my cousin Loles had told me projected itself onto the photo. Though late, her figure had emerged from the blurred background. It had a story. At least for me. And an image, clear, defined. Just like Rosario. In her photo, which must have been taken a few years before the murder, she looked happy, carefree. Nothing had happened yet. And now she was resting in peace alongside her two children.

I needed a minute before I could look at Nicolás's portrait. I had seen his face more than a hundred times in pictures while I was writing the novel. But grave photos are different, even if they come from some ordinary instant, a moment frozen in time. They are the presumptive summation of a life, a representation of it, like first name and last, like the dates of birth and death. Those eyes are the eyes of a cadaver. The last image. The definitive effigy.

Maybe that's why I had to gather my courage before looking at the little oval-shaped photo that was a condensation of Nicolás's existence. His childish face, his bangs over his eyes, took me back briefly to the past. That was his face, timid, reserved, his fleeting, cursory gaze. Yes, that was his face, the face I'd had in front of me so many times. There was no doubt. And yet, something was missing from that photo. Something that Rosi's photo held on to, that their mother's photo preserved too. They were what those images showed. Their photos were definitive. Nicolás's wasn't. He didn't manage to occupy it fully. There was a part of him that wasn't there. That was true in my novel as well. I was certain of that just then: Despite what I'd believed, the invisible presence in the story I had written wasn't Rosi, it was Nicolás. I hadn't known how to make him present. Despite the memories, despite the reflections, despite everything I'd said about him. He remained a shadow. A shifting, vaporous shadow, impossible to pin down.

Something was missing from the photo. Something was missing in my memory too. A scene that would complement that final image. I stood there a while looking at it and tried to conjure up what wasn't there. Then my reflection in the glass fused with the marble plate, and briefly, I saw myself in there, buried, confined in the picture's frame. And at the same time, I saw Nicolás's face fusing with mine. Two worlds interlaced. That vision disconcerted me, and before I knew it, I had stepped aside to try to exorcise my reflection from Nicolás's photo, to get him away from me. That, I think, was when the other gaze broke through, the gaze I had glimpsed once or twice and yet had tried to banish from my memories. His eyes burning when he kicked the ball hard, the rage in him when he won at arm wrestling, when he bit his tongue and didn't know how to stop, when he couldn't calm down, when nothing was a game. . . . When the child disappeared and the monster started to emerge. The monster I never saw completely. The one that broke loose the night the horror occurred. The one that ended Rosi's life.

I had avoided looking at that, had pushed it out of my imagination, had unconsciously enveloped it in a thick fog, white noise, interference. I hadn't wanted to see it until then. I hadn't been able to. But at the cemetery, in the oblique reflection of my outline in the glass panel on the crypt, I saw it break loose all at once. It had the grainy texture of a home movie, a video with choppy sound. A precarious, obscene representation now forming clearly in my mind: the monster, raging, insane, lifting the giant tape player high, beating Rosi with it over and over, harder and harder, furious, biting his tongue, clenching his jaw, not resting between blows, like a robot on an assembly line, like a rabid animal, like a dog that's smelled blood. Then, her body on the ground, disfigured, lifeless. And the monster fleeing. But still present. Walking softly toward the doorbell to disconnect it. Cold. A few seconds. Before disappearing and making way for Nicolás. The anguish, the terror, the cowardice, the drive off, the dark night, the tribulation, the dilemma, the leap, the end of the world.

That was how it had happened. I saw it that morning with a clarity I had never before glimpsed. There was the image I was missing. The monster.

Only later did I realize that what I had imagined was not so far from what Rosario had believed her entire life. That monster was the same thing she'd imagined when she said someone had broken into her house, killing her Rosi and taking her Nicolás away. Because that hadn't been her son. It hadn't been my friend. It had been the monster.

The difference is that I knew, or thought I knew, that monsters don't exist. At least not apart from the people who carry them inside. And so I forced myself, so far as I was able, to link the two images together. My friend and what I had just envisaged. To connect their two gazes, to stare into one and then the other, to saturate them. To produce the definitive image that would capture the essence of Nicolás's existence. To make him visible, to pin down what had eluded me. In all possible ways. But I couldn't. Between him and the monster, there was a deep gulf, a zone of infinite shadow impossible to illuminate.

And it was that zone, as I sensed that morning, that indecipherable darkness, that hid the origin of everything. That was where the question that had moved me to write resided. Not why Nicolás killed Rosi. Not how. Not even what was going through his mind. I would never know, even if I hadn't been able to avoid speculating. No, that wasn't the question, at bottom. If I'd started writing, if I'd decided to stir up the past and had spent three years of my life obsessed by this story, it was for another reason, a question I'd never managed to answer. A contradictory and disturbing feeling that had pursued me all those years. An unease that was born the night the horror occurred and that has never completely gone away.

Can we remember with affection someone who has committed the worst of crimes? Is it licit to do so after having understood the other side? Can we love without forgiving? May we take flowers to a murderer's tomb?

I've never known how to answer. The void, the zone of shadow, leaves no room for words or thoughts. But that morning, there was no need of language. I looked at the carnations at the foot of the mausoleum, and reality gave me an answer.

I didn't stay in the cemetery much longer. Before I left, I prayed an Our Father. It was involuntary. I prayed the way I had prayed with Nicolás so many times. The words now meant nothing to me, but maybe they had some significance for my body, for my memory. They bubbled up inside me like a mantra from the past. The child I was returned briefly. He stood before his friend's grave. And I knew then clearly that nothing ever fully disappears, not good and not evil, that the past remains and accompanies us forever, like a shadow we cannot always make out.

I returned home with the feeling that the story was finally over. The amen of the Our Father I had prayed in the cemetery drew it to a close. The novel, and that long period of obsession. And yet I wasn't at peace. The wound hadn't healed. The phantoms were still with me. I hadn't managed to exorcise them. But I consoled myself with the thought that now, I could at least look them in the eye.

Before bed, I opened the file of the novel, sketched out this chapter, and scrolled through the more than two hundred pages I had written. I read again the phrase that had started it all: *Twenty years ago, on Christmas Eve, my best friend killed his sister and threw himself off a cliff.* Those words held a story. Yes, there was a novel there. A novel full of questions without answers, renunciations, disappointments, frustrated endings, unexpected re-beginnings. A novel of minimal certainties and little glimmers of dust. The novel I had written to learn what was the novel I needed to write.

That was when I started over, and wrote this book through to the end. Not to go down other roads or look for better answers, not to correct errors or keep myself from going astray. I wrote to attest to this shipwreck, to return to the same place and keep losing myself, to fail again, to maybe fail better.

EPILOGUE

I FINISHED WRITING this novel in May of 2017. The day I sent the manuscript to my agent, I managed to breathe easy. I was free, and slowly, I could return to my life. I tried to turn the page and forget the story that had obsessed me in recent years. And I almost did. I even ceased to be worried by the possible consequences of what I had written. I knew—I know—that literature isn't innocuous, that it causes collateral damage, especially when it concerns flesh-and-blood people who haven't asked to be a part of it. But I was convinced that I had written the book I had to write, and I thought I was prepared for whatever might come.

When summer passed, though, and I knew the book would see the light of day, the self-assurance I had felt when I'd sent off the manuscript disappeared, and I started to doubt everything again. Then the nightmares returned. Rosi and Nicolás were in them, and their parents and brothers too. They harangued me and I apologized, but they wouldn't listen. In the morning I'd rise feeling awful, riddled with guilt it was hard for me to suppress.

In those weeks, I dreamed of Juan Alberto several times. Those dreams weren't as raw as the ones with

Rosi and Nicolás, but I did argue with him, and I would wake in sorrow. I knew that I was still disturbed by the thought that the story might hurt him.

For that reason, perhaps, before sending the final version to the publisher, I gathered the courage to call him and gave him a copy of the manuscript. It was too late to change anything, but I needed to make clear to him why I'd written what I had. Our friendship was one of the few things I was unwilling to risk for the sake of literature.

Instead of meeting near the university or at any of the countless cafes in Murcia, I said we should go to El Yeguas. I arrived fifteen minutes early and waited for him with a coffee with milk at the bar. As I was texting him to tell him I was there, someone shook me from behind, and I nearly dropped my phone.

"What the fuck, kid, you get lost or something?"

I had never been with Garre without one of my brothers around, and I didn't know how to react. I prayed Juan Alberto wouldn't take too long.

Garre ordered a coffee with brandy and settled down next to me at the bar.

"You want me to bless it?" he asked, pushing a bottle of brandy close to my cup.

"No thanks."

"Of course not. Intellectuals."

I smiled, more or less.

"Tell me then?" he asked, doctoring his own coffee until it nearly overflowed. "How's it going with that book you've been writing?"

"It's done," I said, pointing at the bound manuscript lying on the bar.

Without asking for permission, he grabbed it and weighed it in his hands. "So you wrote all this? Three hundred pages? That's a hell of a lot of work, kid."

He wasn't being ironic. Not that I could tell, anyway. To the contrary, I detected something resembling admiration at my effort in his words.

"You're in it," I said.

"Get the fuck out. Now I'm going to have to end up reading the damn thing."

The two of us laughed.

"So? You find anything out?" he asked.

"Some things. But I never managed to consult the..."

"Sh," he cut me off. "Don't spoil the ending. Not when I've gotten interested in a book for the first time in my life."

I smiled. I was having a normal conversation with Garre. I wouldn't have minded talking to him for the rest of the afternoon.

When Juan Alberto arrived, Garre stepped off, saying goodbye with an enthusiastic handshake.

"Hey, kid," he added, "we'll see if you don't start coming around here more now. Nobody's going to bite. And you, try to get outside more, you could use a bit of sun. You look like a goddamn vampire."

This last comment was for Juan Alberto, who gave him a perplexed look before cracking up. I think it was then that I began to understand Garre's sarcasm. Maybe my brothers hadn't been so wrong about him.

Juan Alberto and I walked to the dining room and chose a table to sit down.

"Here? Next to your altar?" he asked, referring to a press clipping on the wall with my photo.

"We'll be more protected here," I joked.

I didn't drag out the small talk, and after ordering a chamomile tea for him and another coffee for myself, I handed him the manuscript.

He turned the pages attentively, and stopped on the photograph of the cliff.

"That's you," I said. "That's your green tracksuit."

"Fucking hell, Miguel," he exclaimed.

And immediately, he started crying.

Like a reflex, my eyes filled with tears too.

Juan Alberto waited a few seconds in silence for his grief to abate. And I waited for him to speak.

And after that pause, as though a switch had been flipped inside him, Juan Alberto told me all the things he had never told me before. How he got word at five in the morning of what had happened, how he ran through the fields until he found his cousin's body, how he couldn't sleep for months, how he too decided to run away and not think about that moment, how he had failed to escape it entirely, and how, every time he saw me, something of those days, and even of that night, flared up again and burned him inside.

Maybe that was the key to everything. There, condensed, was all that grief. All that we had never told each other. All that was left unsaid and was less important than the fact that it could be said. The words that, for once, I am not prepared to turn into literature. A conversation between two friends. Twenty-three years after the fact. A bit of life among so much writing.

When Juan Alberto left, I stayed a while at the bar. I took out the black notebook I was carrying and wrote down what I had just experienced.

Antolín came over and asked if everything was all right.

"Everything's perfect," I responded, and I ordered a beer and a snack of potato salad and anchovy.

I settled into my chair, looked back at my notebook, and was surprised by how the words began to flow. It was the first time in my entire life I'd gone to El Yeguas without any of my brothers. At the next table over, some locals had started a game of dominos. The violent crack of the tiles on the metal table, which had startled me so many times, now no longer seemed deafening. It wasn't even strange. It formed part of the image that I lived in. My hipster cap, my plastic-framed glasses didn't attract anyone's attention. Nor did the notebook on the table. When all was said and done, I was the son of Emilia, Juan Antonio's youngest, the brother of the sculptor. And sure, I was about to finish a novel. But that was what mattered least.

THE COFFINS MOVE into the distance, the chapel is empty. This is the end of what began two days before. A long night, infinite. You think, naively, that now it's all over.

You return home, you feel vertigo, and you shut yourself away to study. Your brain is full of temples, pyramids, and sculptures, and that takes you away from where you are.

The days pass, and you return to college. We saw you on TV, your classmates and friends tell you. February will come, and you will pass your exams with honors. Four years later, you'll finish your degree and get a scholarship. You'll end up being a professor at the same school where you studied. You'll leave the lowlands and marry the woman you love. Your parents will die, and the house will be abandoned. You'll write a novel and meet authors you admire. You'll tell the story of the murder to a writer who's also a friend. He'll tell you that's the story you're looking for. You'll start writing it and will return to the past. Twenty years later, Nicolás will return to your life. You'll remember that dark night and will try to pass through it. You'll fail over and over, and you'll have to start anew.

You'll return then to these scattered notes. You'll give shape to the scribbles you threw in the garbage before. You'll understand that the wall of fog will never dissipate, that the bitter night will remain anchored in time. But you'll also sense at last what is throbbing on the other side of the mist. You'll discover then the cracks that the light filters through. And you'll understand for the first time how much words matter. The words that hurt and the words that save. The words written in a notebook, the words whispered in an ear. The words held fast in the soul and the ones that take half a life to arrive.

PHOTO CREDITS

"Group of People in a Cart with a Pony." Undated. Courtesy of the author's archive.

"Cliff." Photo from *La Verdad*, 12/26/1995. © Tito Bernal. Courtesy of the Archivo Regional de Murcia.

"Group of People." Photo from *La Verdad*, 12/26/1995. © Tito Bernal. Courtesy of the Archivo Regional de Murcia.

Munchausen's Visit, 1987. © Francesc Torres. Courtesy of the artist.

Screen grab from the morning news on TVE Murcia, 12/26/1995. Courtesy of RTVE Murcia.

The Eyes of Gutete Emerita, 1996. © Alfredo Jaar. Courtesy of the artist.

ABOUT THE AUTHOR

Miguel Ángel Hernández is a Spanish writer best known for his works of fiction, among them the novels *Intento de escapada* (2013), which won the Premio Ciudad Alcalá de Narrativa and was translated into five languages, and *El instante de peligro* (2015), which was a finalist for the Premio Herralde de Novela. *El dolor de los demás*—the original Spanish-language edition of *The Pain of Others*—was selected in 2018 as a book of the year by *El País* and the *New York Times en Español.* Hernández teaches art history at the University of Murcia and has authored several books on art and visual culture. His novel *Anoxia* was published by Other Press in 2025.

ABOUT THE TRANSLATOR

Adrian Nathan West is a writer and literary critic based in Spain. He has translated more than twenty books, among them Rainald Goetz's *Insane*, Sibylle Lacan's *A Father: Puzzle*, and Sergi Pàmies's *The Art of Wearing a Trench Coat* (Other Press, 2021).